Praise for *Flight of Deception*

"Delightful! Flight of Deception is another fast paced Mike Paull mystery that keeps the reader t̶̶̶ ̶̶̶ages. The thrilling sequel to Flight of B̶̶̶ ̶̶̶ ̶̶̶vists and turns of Brett and ̶̶̶ ̶̶̶emingly insurmountable od̶̶̶ ̶̶̶ell-told tale of intrigue shou̶̶̶ ̶̶̶fan."

Jam̶̶̶ ̶̶̶author of the ̶̶̶ick Grant Adventures series

...

"Author Mike Paull has served up another exciting Brett Raven Saga. The sequel to Flight of Betrayal continues to tell the mystery, with well-developed characters and a convoluted but believable plot. Flight of Deception is a well-researched, intriguing story. This book will urge the reader to continue, page after page, until the end. Then he'll want more..."

JR Hafer, aviation writer
20thCenturyAviationMagazine.com

...

"Flight of Deception continues the mystery series of Brett Raven. Mike Paull has once again proven he is among a handful of authors who can weave flying adventures into a mystery novel and make it believable. The novel is just convoluted enough to keep the reader wondering where it is leading and when he finds out, wondering how it will possibly end."

C.K. Griswold, mystery novel editor

ALSO BY MIKE PAULL

Flight of Betrayal
Tales from the Sky Kitchen Café

Praise for *Flight of Betrayal*

"The book sucks you in, as good mysteries do, and when it is over, you find yourself wanting to hear more from this author. Now I am waiting, as I expect all of the readers will be, for the next book. Because I still have questions that need answers...

Amber Abney, Upgraded Living Magazine

•••

"The tale is satisfyingly convoluted, the sex tender, the hero someone worth rooting for. It's great fun."

Dan Barnett, Chico Enterprise Record

•••

Praise for *Tales from the Sky Kitchen Cafe*

"This is a different sort of book. Mike uses the backdrop of the Sky Kitchen Café, where his subjects met every day, to illustrate through words, the friendship and brotherhood between the men and women in his stories. The author has successfully written a series of aviation based stories in a language which allows readers with no background in the subject to understand and enjoy them."

Walter J. Boyne, Author, Historian, and Former Director National Air and Space Museum

•••

"The author has a very pleasantly fluid and entertaining style. He develops each of the short stories in a way that brings the reader through the experience of each of the pilots as if they were your friend as well. You become a part of the elite group as if you were having coffee with them."

Joseph J. Gleason, 20thCenturyAviationMagazine.com

FLIGHT OF DECEPTION

MIKE PAULL

Published by Skyhawk Publishing

Printed in the USA

Design by Carla Resnick

ISBN 9780985874322

Library of Congress Catalog Number 2013914355

FLIGHT OF DECEPTION

To my good buddy, Mike Dakof, who

encouraged me to write, but never got to

read my books.

"The true mystery of the world is the visible, not the invisible."

—Oscar Wilde

FLIGHT OF DECEPTION

PROLOGUE

Ten to fifteen years in Federal Prison... That was the penalty in the year 2000 for committing insurance fraud by faking a death.

Besides his new wife Maria, Brett and Annie were the only people who knew J.T. Talbot had faked his own death so that he and Maria could collect $5.5 million in fraudulent insurance benefits. Unfortunately, Brett and Annie had also received over $5 million dollars in swindled funds. They wanted to return all the money to the insurance companies, but how?

One would think it a simple task to give the money back, but it wasn't. Brett and Annie were trapped between a rock and a hard place. They knew J.T. was alive. It was his supposed death in a plane crash which had brought Annie a life insurance payout of $5 million, and Brett a payout of almost $200 thousand for the loss of his airplane. If Brett divulged all the information he possessed, exposed the crime, and returned the funds, he would open himself up to retaliation from gangsters in Mexico. If he didn't, the insurance companies would think he and Annie were accomplices to the fraud and were only returning the money because they had gotten cold feet.

CHAPTER 1

Brett was on his second cup of coffee and the back page of the sports section by the time Annie came down the stairs from the bedroom and poured herself a cup. "Are we out of cream?" she inquired.

"It's over here on the counter."

Annie sat down and stirred the half and half into her coffee. "How did you sleep?"

He laughed. "Before or after?"

"Sorry I woke you, but the urge came over me."

"Hey, don't apologize, it was great. I don't remember it being that good when we were married. You been reading some 'how to' books?"

Annie sipped her coffee while holding the cup

in both hands. "That doesn't say much for the old days."

Brett winced, "I meant it as a compliment not a criticism."

"I know. A lot has changed since we were first married twenty years ago."

Brett smiled and changed the subject before he got in over his head. "I'm driving up to San Francisco this afternoon for the meeting with the lawyer. How 'bout you take the train up and we'll go out to dinner."

"What time will the meeting be over?"

"I'm getting there at three thirty, should be out around five."

"You pick me up at the station?" Annie asked, as she drained the last of the coffee from her cup.

"Sure."

Annie dissected the front page from the pile of papers. "Where we going?"

"How about the Waterfront, I could really go for some Sand Dabs."

Annie was searching for page three. "What did you do to this paper?"

"Sorry, I messed it up a little. What about dinner?" Brett asked again.

"Okay, I'll take the four-thirty."

Brett pulled up in front of the Southern Pacific station just before five-thirty. Annie waved and hustled to the car before any restless drivers could lean on their horns. She looked great. She wore jeans, a black blazer, and red opened toed pumps which raised her from an even five feet to almost five two. She jumped in.

Brett leaned over and gave her a kiss on the lips. "Man, do you smell good. What is it?"

"It's called Wish; just came out last year. 1999 was a good year for perfume."

"Fruit?"

"No, vanilla. Oriental, no less."

"Mmm," Brett whispered as he ran his tongue across the side of her neck. "Tastes good too."

She laughed and shoved his head away. "Not here, the guy behind us is giving you the finger."

Brett looked in the rear view mirror, laughed and pulled away from the curb. He merged onto the Embarcadero and in ten minutes pulled up in front of Pier Seven. A valet parking attendant opened the door for Annie and said, "Welcome to the Waterfront."

Brett took the claim check from the blond haired young man, who looked as if he had just walked out of a Beach Boys movie, and slipped a five dollar bill into his hand. "See if you can put it where it won't get dinged. It's brand new."

Brett put his arm around Annie's waist and held her close as they slipped through the door into the restaurant. They were early, so with no competition for tables, the hostess led them to one near the window. Brett gave Annie the seat with a direct view of the Bay Bridge and he took the one facing Alcatraz. "Martini?" Brett asked.

"Great," Annie said, as she smeared a wad of unsalted butter over a piece of heavy crusted sourdough, that had already been placed on the table.

When the waiter returned, Brett ordered the drinks. "Two Tanqueray Martinis up, dry, with the olives on the side." He ripped a piece of bread off the loaf and devoured the crust.

"How'd the meeting go?" Annie asked.

"Good, I told him the whole story."

"What'd he say about your plan to recover all the insurance money?"

Brett paused as the waiter set the drinks in front of them. "Cheers," he said as they tapped glasses and let the warm liquid slide down their throats.

Annie set down her glass and chewed on an olive. "So what about your plan?"

"He liked the idea, but didn't want to know all the details. Just in case we cross the line, he wanted to be removed from it, but he'll handle the negotiations with the insurance companies for us."

The waiter returned. Annie ordered a lettuce wedge with blue cheese and broiled salmon. Brett went for a Caesar and as anticipated, the Sand Dabs.

Annie looked concerned. "What do you mean, cross the line?"

"Come on, Annie, you know we'll be walking a tightrope."

"Yeah, but is it illegal?"

"That's an interesting question. If you steal money that was stolen from someone else and return it back to its rightful owner, is it a crime or a good deed?"

"I'm scared," Annie said while separating another piece of sourdough from the loaf.

Brett reached across the table and put his right hand over Annie's — his left one still had a cast on it. "You don't have to be in on this you know. I can keep you away from it."

"I want to be there with you. I'm not going to let you carry this burden all by yourself. You did that when you discovered the truth about the plane crash and you didn't have anyone to lean on."

He squeezed her hands. "You're in then?'

"Yes, I'm scared, but I'm in."

The food arrived and they ate in silence for five minutes. Then Annie asked, "Is he going to get the agreements from the Insurance companies?"

"His name is Vince. He's pretty sure they'll go for it. We get their ten and a half million back and they close the case."

"What about the recovery fee?"

"Vince knows without that, there's no deal. Dessert?"

"Just coffee."

Brett ordered two double decaf espressos. "Annie, it's going to work."

She forced a smile.

Brett nibbled on a biscotti that had been served on the saucer with the coffee. "Can I change the subject?"

"Sure."

"Let's get married again."

Annie almost choked on her coffee. "Brett, we've only been back together for a little over a month."

"It's not like we don't know each other, we were married for fifteen years."

Annie thought for a moment and then said, "Brett, it's just too soon. I love you but I'm not ready to be remarried."

"Do you think you'll ever be ready?"

"Maybe, but I still have issues that I have to resolve.

"Can I help you resolve them?"

"It's not about you, it's about me. I can't talk about marriage yet, besides, I have to get a legal divorce from J.T. before I can marry anybody."

"That's going to be hard since he's legally dead."

"I know; I have an appointment with a divorce attorney on Friday. Problem is I don't know what to tell him about J.T."

"Just tell him the truth. He married Maria under an assumed name while he was still married to you."

Annie took a bite from her cookie. "It's so bizarre and so embarrassing."

"Annie, it's not your fault. J.T. betrayed you, not the other way around."

"I know, but there's a sense of shame that comes along with it, especially when he left me a bogus $5 million life insurance policy; as if that would absolve him. All he really left was a couple hundred thousand dollars in overdue bills."

Brett nodded in agreement and then changed the subject back to them. "Are the issues you're dealing with still related to when I talked you into the abortion?"

"Brett, I've already forgiven you for that. I just have to be sure I've forgiven myself. I keep thinking about the plans we made twenty years ago when we were in college."

"You mean the house with the white picket fence and the three kids running barefoot in the yard?"

"Exactly; twenty years has matured me enough to know those young dreams don't always come true, but now that I'm in my forties and living with the realization I can never have children..."

Brett interrupted, "Annie, let me help you work through that."

"Brett, I need you to listen to me for a change without trying to solve the problem. Just listen."

Brett was silent and Annie went on. "I want to solve my own problems. Our relationship will never be right if I let you solve all the problems, make all the decisions, and I just come along for the ride."

"I'm sorry," he said. "Even though I'm trying hard, I fall back into those old habits. Will you let me know if I can help?"

Annie put her hands over his. "Brett, I know you want to help me and I love you for it, but just don't help so much."

"I think I understand," he whispered softly

"You can start by not pressuring me about marriage. Promise me you won't pressure me."

"Okay, I just have to know though, if you think you'll ever be ready."

"I don't know; I hope so."

Brett was silent as he fiddled with the cookie crumbs on the table and then he said, "I know I'm making most of the decisions about this insurance money. Am I overpowering you with that also?"

"Brett, I understand that you need to do this and I'm good with it. We've talked and you've let me in on everything that's going to happen. This is your deal and I'm fine with you being the quarterback. Just don't forget I'm on the team."

"I won't, I really want you with me on this," he said, as he signaled the waiter for their check.

CHAPTER 2

Vince Moreno was a partner in the firm of Roberts, Moreno and Fisk. The entire firm specialized in insurance law, and they were considered the best on the West Coast.

Vince was on a first name basis with most of the insurance companies' CEO's and district managers. This Monday morning he called Connecticut Mutual Life and asked to speak to Ralph Phillips, the Western United States manager.

A young female voice asked, "Who may I tell Mr. Phillips is calling?"

"Vince Moreno. He knows me."

"Thank you, Mr. Moreno, may I place you on hold?"

"Sure, but don't be gone too long."

It took less than a minute and the secretary was back. "I have Mr. Phillips, go ahead."

A loud booming voice came through the earpiece. "Vince, it's been awhile. Why do I have the pleasure this morning?"

Vince smiled into the mouthpiece in order to keep his voice soft and pleasant. "I'd like to say it was just a social call, but I have an important matter that I need to discuss with you. Connecticut Mutual may be able to recover several million dollars from a claim they recently paid."

Ralph Phillips tone became pure business. "I don't suppose we can do this on the phone."

"We're going to need a meeting, and we're going to need a manager from Ohio Life and General Aviation Insurance to join us."

"How big a recovery are we talking about?"

Vince paused for about fifteen seconds; he wanted Ralph on the end of his chair. "Over ten million."

"How much of it is ours?"

"Let's wait and I'll fill everyone in at once."

"Okay Vince, let's schedule it for nine a.m. this coming Friday at the San Francisco office. I'll make sure the other two companies will be here."

"Sounds great. By the way, have a lawyer from each company there also."

Ralph laughed, "And I actually thought this

might be social call. See you Friday."

The San Francisco office of Connecticut Mutual Life occupied the entire twenty second floor of the Transamerica Building, commonly referred to by locals as the Pyramid.

Vince was intentionally fifteen minutes late; he wanted all of the players at the table when he arrived. He wore a pinstripe, double breasted, blue suit with a red tie and carried a brown briefcase full of documents. Following close behind him was a junior lawyer from his firm who also wore a blue pinstripe and carried a black briefcase.

A pretty brunette in high heels, a very short skirt, and a tight sweater greeted them and showed them to the conference room, where already seated in their suits and ties were the three managers and their lawyers. A stenographer was seated at a small secondary table with a computer in front of her. Coffee and pastries were being passed by a secretary as Vince and his assistant took their seats in the middle of the long mahogany table. Ralph Phillips took charge and introduced all the participants, then turned the meeting over to Vince.

Vince loved this part. All the managers and their lawyers were trying to be nonchalant, but he knew their curiosity was high and they were eager to hear what he had to say. He shuffled through his papers as if looking for a document. In reality he was letting the suspense build before he began.

He pulled a document from his case, glanced down at it and stood up to address the other men. He liked having his audience looking up at him. "Gentlemen, on March 12th of this year a small twin engine airplane crashed in Baja Mexico near San Felipe and the bodies of two men were incinerated. That crash cost Connecticut Mutual $5 million, Ohio Life $4.25 million, and General Aviation Insurance $1.44 million. The total insurance loss that day was over $10.5 million."

The room was quiet except for the hum of the stenographer's computer, and Vince's words lingered in the air as thick as the fog outside the window. "I have clients who discovered a fraud and can recover at least $10.5 million of your losses; however, there are three conditions." He paused for a sip of water and then continued. "First, they need a guarantee that they will not be accused of, or prosecuted for, any crime. Second, they need a six month window to recover the entire ten and a half million. Today is the first of October, which would put their deadline at the end of March."

Ralph Phillips chimed in. "I don't suppose they are doing this because of their love for insurance companies."

Vince laughed. "No, not at all; however, this brings us to the third condition. When my clients deliver the funds, you will agree to pay them a 10% recovery fee."

The lawyer from Ohio life decided to join the discussion. "It sounds to me like your clients were involved in stealing our money and now they want to get paid for returning it."

"I know it looks that way, but it's not what happened. My clients received a portion of your payouts in good faith. It wasn't until later they discovered a fraud had been perpetrated and the money they received was not due them."

The lawyer spoke up again. "So why don't they just give us the money back?"

"I just told you the reason. They're afraid you will try to implicate them in the crime."

Now the General Aviation attorney was all over Vince. "So they want us to pay them 10% to give back the money."

Vince knew this question was coming. "No, they'll give you their $5.2 million back without any fees. If you want the entire $10.5 million back, it will cost you 10% of the full amount."

Ralph Phillips asked, "How do they justify that?"

"You guys have to realize they have spent a lot of time and money, not to mention personal risk, to solve a case that you had no idea even existed. In addition in order to recover your entire loss, they'll need to expend more money, more time and expose themselves to additional personal risk."

One of the lawyers was back in. "Sounds like a shake down to me."

My clients are not trying to shake down any insurance companies. You hire investigators all the time to do exactly this. They nose around, find out if insurance fraud took place, and if it did, recover the funds. It's your choice; you can get the five mil back immediately and it will cost you nothing, or you can pay a fee and recover the entire ten and a half mil."

The same lawyer said, "It sounds like they don't know where the second five and a half million is. What if they're unable to locate it?"

"Then you get the first five mill back, kiss my clients on the forehead, and the case is closed."

"What about the perpetrators?" The Manager of General Aviation asked. "Are your clients going to deliver them?"

Vince made eye contact with each of the men at the table. "Look guys, my clients aren't detectives and they're not cops. If you want the bad guys arrested, you track 'em down and put the cuffs on them. Only problem is you might not get the money."

Ralph Phillips rose to his feet. "Vince, I think we need to discuss this between ourselves. There's fresh coffee in the lounge."

Vince turned to his young associate, "Jim, would you distribute the docs."

Jim almost popped a button on his jacket as he jumped to his feet and began dropping a package of agreements in front of each of the executives and their lawyers.

Vince closed his briefcase and started for the door with Jim scurrying behind. "Gentlemen, I know you have the authority to make this decision without sending it upstairs. We can stick around for an hour, but if you need longer than that, I'll report to my clients that you aren't interested."

Ralph frowned, "Vince, an hour isn't a long time."

"Come on gentlemen, it's a no brainer and you know it. An hour is about fifty-nine minutes too long. We'll be in the lounge." Jim closed the door behind them.

CHAPTER 3

It was Monday morning and Brett was at his office at 9 a.m. sharp. He came in every day from nine to twelve, even though he wasn't able to work on any of his dental patients. A month earlier, while tracking J.T., he had been attacked by two goons working for Mexican black marketeers and they had inflicted enough damage to his left hand that he was unable to practice. John Gruber was doing a good job filling in for him; however, Brett wanted the patients to know he was on the mend and would eventually be returning to the practice; therefore, he made sure he was visible in the office everyday

Ginger looked up from her reception desk.

"Well, well, the one armed dentist is here and right on time. What did the doctor say at your exam?"

"Looks like at least another four months. The cast has to stay on for another sixty days."

Ginger nodded her approval and said, "I know it's none of my business, but are you and Annie back together?"

Brett smiled; everything that had anything to do with Brett or the office was Ginger's business. "Yeah, she moved her stuff in a few weeks ago."

Ginger wanted more. "Is she going to keep J.T.'s last name or is she going back to yours and be Annie Raven again?"

"Well, even though we used to be married, we're not married now. It's up to her, but I'm guessing she'll go back to her maiden name, Annie Frazier."

Ginger gave it some thought and again nodded her approval. "That makes sense. The name Talbot never seemed right for her."

Brett changed the subject. "The mail here from over the weekend?"

Ginger scooped up a three inch pile of envelopes and a four inch pile of newsletters and journals. "Make sure you throw out the junk, I'll take the bills. By the way you had a phone call this morning. A guy named Biff Erskine left you a message. Said he's an investigator for some insurance company. Sounds like a character from Death of a Salesman."

Brett felt a knot tie in his stomach. "Did he say what he was calling about?"

"No, but he wasn't very polite. Left his number;

said 'make sure he calls me back' and hung up."

Brett took the mail and the message and strolled back to his private office. The treatment rooms were full with two hygienists busy scraping teeth, and Dr. Gruber buried inside a patient's mouth. "I wonder if they even miss me," he mumbled to himself as he opened the door to his office.

He sat down at his desk and started to open the mail, but he kept glancing at the message. *Biff Erskine - 415-555-2777. Call back this a.m.*

The buzz from the intercom jolted him from his thoughts. He pushed the lighted button on the phone panel, "What is it Ginger?"

"Annie's on line two."

"Thanks, I'll get it."

He switched to the other line. "Hi, what's up?"

Annie sounded upset, "I just had a call from an insurance investigator."

"His name Biff?"

"Yes, how'd you know?"

"I got one too. What did you say to him?"

"Told him I couldn't talk right now. Said I'd get back to him."

"Good, are you at the house?"

"Yes, I was on my way out when he called."

"Stay there, I'll be home in ten minutes."

Brett and Annie had bought the townhouse in the hills of San Carlos back in 1985 when they were married. After their divorce ten years later, Annie married J.T., Brett's airplane partner and best friend. She gave the house to Brett, but when

J.T. ended up betraying both of them, Annie moved back with Brett.

It only took Brett five minutes to drive the mile and half up the hill. As usual he admired the view of the San Francisco Bay Area as he walked from the parking area to his front door. It was a clear day and he could see all the way from San Francisco to San Jose.

Annie was at the door waiting anxiously. "What are we going to do?"

"Come on, sit down, we're not going to panic. Our plan isn't going to change just because some investigator is nosing around. You didn't use any of the insurance proceeds to pay off any of J.T.'s bills did you?"

Annie flopped down in an overstuffed chair and Brett took a seat on the couch. "No way, I had the $200 thousand in alimony money you had paid me over the last five years. It wrung me dry, but I used most of that money to pay off all the bills J.T. had run up before he was killed… or supposedly killed in the airplane accident. The $5 million is in three different bank accounts."

Brett looked relieved. "That's good; I put my $190 thousand in a separate account also."

Annie looked worried, "Brett, I thought Vince Moreno cut us a deal."

Brett nodded in agreement, "He did, let's find out what's going on."

CHAPTER 4

Brett dialed the number for Roberts, Moreno and Fisk. A pleasant voice answered, "Law offices."

"Vince Moreno, please, it's Brett Raven."

Elevator music played as Brett waited for Vince to pick up. Finally a click produced Vince's voice, "Brett, what's up?"

"Hey, Vince, both Annie and I had a call from an insurance investigator. I thought we had the okay to push ahead with our plan."

"They signed all the agreements Brett; they can't renege at this point. Where are you, I'll give a call and get back."

"I'm home, you have the number."

"Sit tight; I won't be more than an hour."

Ralph Phillips was in a meeting and Vince was told he would return his call within the next thirty minutes. When his secretary put through the call, Vince answered without the usual smile in his voice, "Ralph, what the fuck? We have a signed deal with you and the other two companies and now I find out you have an investigator nosing around."

"Vince, none of the agreements prohibit us from doing some investigation."

Vince tried to control his temper. "Only problem is that this guy might muck up the works."

"We may have to take that chance. If our guy gets the missing five mill back, we only have to pay him 5% of five million. If your people find it, we have to pay 10% of ten million."

Now Vince was furious. "You realize if this guy scares them off, you'll be out that entire five million. I never took you for a guy who would risk that amount of money just to save a little on the back end."

Ralph was quiet, and then spoke apologetically, "Vince, I'm really sorry. I was against it, but the lawyers from the other two companies are real pricks. They convinced their guys that you were screwing 'em. Young studs who justify their salary by making big decisions, even when they're stupid ones."

"Ralph, you realize this private dick has no idea what went down in this scam. He's going to turn over some rocks that shouldn't be disturbed. My client's safety may be compromised."

"I was afraid of that and argued against it, but

I got voted down two to one. The agreements still hold; if your people deliver before the investigator, they get their money."

"I know that, but this guy will be in the way."

"This is just between you and me. If your clients need my help, have them contact me. I'll help with whatever they need."

"Okay, thanks, Ralph. They're going to get you your money, I can almost guarantee it."

Brett picked up on the first ring. "Vince?"

"Yeah, Brett it's me. Your agreements are still good. Only thing is, two of the companies think they'll get more bang for their buck with the P.I. You're going to have to do your thing while dancing around him."

"Should we ignore him?"

"I'd talk to him, see if he knows anything. You might even want to make him think you'll help him. Just keep him chasing his tail."

"Okay, thanks Vince. Anything else?"

"Oh yeah, the manager from Connecticut Mutual Life, Ralph Phillips, is on your side. If you need his help you can trust him. "

Brett hung up the phone. Annie was waiting, "So?"

"So I guess we call Biff Erskine back."

CHAPTER 5

Both Brett and Annie responded nervously to the stiff knock on the front door. Annie opened it and motioned the investigator to come in.

Biff Erskine wasn't an attractive guy. He stood about six feet five, towering over Brett by a half foot. He carried about three hundred and seventy-five pounds on that frame, but unfortunately, at least fifty of them were hanging over his belt. He had a jagged scar across his cheek and his crew cut was military style — short and ugly. His eyes were steel gray giving him an angry look even when he smiled, which wasn't very often.

He handed his card to Brett who looked at it and passed it on to Annie; she read it, shrugged, and handed it back.

**Elmer "Biff" Erskine
Private Investigations
Specializing in insurance fraud
415-555-2777**

"Mind if I ask you a few questions?" he said in a tone designed for intimidation.

"Mind if I tell you to go fuck yourself?" Brett responded, unintimidated.

Biff tried to force a smile, but it came out as a smirk. "Look buddy, I'm just trying to make a buck doing my job."

"And what is that job, exactly?"

"I discover fraud, identify perps, and recover money for insurance companies."

"Really, how does that work? You find the bad guys and bring them in strapped over the hood of your pickup truck?" Biff tried to smile again, but his lips just wouldn't go there. "You on a flat fee or percentage?" Brett continued.

"Look, Raven, cut the act. You know exactly how it works. I'm told you're my competitor and you want a big piece of the action."

Brett motioned toward the living room. "How about a beer, Elmer?"

Biff's face flushed red. "Sure I'll take one, and by the way I go by the name of Biff."

Brett took the card out of his pocket, gave it a glance, shrugged and feigned bewilderment. "Sure, Biff, for a minute I thought I read it wrong."

Annie said, "I'll get them" and headed for the

fridge.

Brett sat on one end of the couch and saved the other end for Annie. Biff was steered toward one of the arm chairs that faced the sofa, which he squeezed into, and molded himself to the sides like a wad of silly putty. Annie returned, handed Biff a Pale Ale, set one down for Brett and another for herself.

"So what makes you think I'm in competition with you?" Brett asked.

Biff took a long slug from the bottle and drained half the bronze liquid from it. He gave a hearty belch and said, "I know about the deal you made with the companies."

Annie stepped in. "If we're your competitors why the hell do you think we'd feed you any information?"

Biff finished the beer with one more gulp and tapped his chest with his fist to hold down another burp. "I was thinking we could maybe partner up, share information, and split the commission."

Brett broke into laughter. "Elm... I mean Biff; you don't have any idea what this case is about, do you? You don't have any information to share. You're here to get info, not share it."

"I may not have much yet, but I'll have it soon enough and when I get it I'll run with it. If you're in my way, I'll run right over you."

Brett was unimpressed. "Look Biff, we're not on a football field or a Marine Corps bivouac. This is going to be a brain game not a brawn one. I hope you've got enough gray matter upstairs to keep up with it."

Biffs face flushed crimson and it looked like the top of his head might blow off. "I've been down this road lots of times and faced off with wise guys smarter than you, and I always came out the winner."

Brett didn't flinch. "Have you ever heard the expression, 'past performance is no indication of future success?' You're in way over your head on this one."

The normal color returned to Biff's cheeks. "I'll tell you what I do know. The insurance companies think both of you were involved in a scam. The Mrs. here collected $5 million for the death of her husband, a guy named J.T. Talbot. Only thing is he's still alive. And you collected almost $200 thousand for the replacement of an airplane you co-owned with him before he destroyed it."

Brett edged closer to Biff and looked him straight in the eyes. "You have any evidence he's alive?"

Biff pushed his chair back a couple inches. "No."

"If he is alive, you know where he is?"

"No."

"Any idea who the second guy in the plane was?"

"Yeah, his name's Russo. He's apparently alive too. His wife collected on two policies. That's the five and half million we're all after."

"You have any evidence he's alive?"

"No.

"If he is alive, any idea where he is?"

"No."

Brett pulled back from Biff. "Elmer, you don't have 'jack'. I think this meeting's over. Give us a call when you have some information to share with us; then maybe we'll talk about partnering up."

Biff disengaged himself from the chair and started for the door. "I'm a fast learner. I'm gonna have the answers soon and I'm gonna beat you to that $5.5 million. And my name's Biff."

Brett opened the door and said. "Good luck, Biff. You're gonna need it."

CHAPTER 6

Brett and Annie were determined to recover as much as they could of the five and a half million J.T. had swindled from the insurance companies. Before they could implement Brett's plan, however, they had to locate where J.T., who was last known as Tony Russo, had fled with his new wife Maria.

Brett had let J.T. and Maria slip through his grasp a month ago in Colorado. He knew they were headed east so Brett began a process of deductive reasoning. J.T. loved the ocean and he hated cold weather. Fleeing to the east would suggest they were headed to the Carolina's, Florida, Georgia or the gulf coast of Alabama, Mississippi, Louisiana, or Texas. Brett had talked often with J.T. when they were friends and airplane partners, about flying their plane through the gulf area. J.T. wasn't too keen on it. He felt, except for New Orleans, that area was full of hick towns. Brett's gut told him to look in the Carolina's or Florida.

Once flying gets into your blood it's like a narcotic and you become addicted. Brett knew J.T. was an addict. It wouldn't be very long before he started looking around for a new airplane and Brett knew which airplane he would look for. The plane they had owned together, the same one which J.T. had sacrificed in Baja, was a twin engine Beechcraft Baron 58. They were both in love with that plane.

Pilots who are looking to buy an airplane, and even those who just enjoy looking, frequent the aircraft sales publications. Brett fired up his iMac and did a search for aircraft sales publications. The number one listed was Trade A Plane; however, it had a huge circulation over the entire United States and Canada. He wanted one that was more regional and kept searching until he spotted the Southeast AeroTrader. It targeted sales in North Carolina, South Carolina, Georgia and Florida. It was also free and was distributed at general aviation airports where interested buyers and sellers could pick up copies in terminals, stores, or repair stations. He jotted down the phone number.

While he had his computer open he typed PHONE NUMBER SERVICES into the search box. To his surprise, dozens of companies popped up. Most of them set up 800 numbers and also temporary phone numbers in any state and almost any city desired. Brett picked one at random with the name, U.S. Calling, and gave them a call. "How does it work?" He asked the sales person. "I need a local phone number with a voicemail attached."

"That's exactly what we do. You pick the local city and state and we'll assign the number. You can record a message in the voicemail and you can access responses from wherever you wish."

Brett was amazed. "I only need it for a month. What are the fees?"

"Since you only need it for thirty days you pay a one-time fee of fifty-nine ninety-five. If you think you might need it for three months we'd give you a good deal for twenty-nine ninety-five a month."

"I hope a month is all I need." Brett thought of something else. "What if I need to make an outgoing call from a local phone number?"

"You phone us and we route it through one of our house numbers. Fifty cents a minute."

"Hang on a minute." Brett pulled an atlas out of his bookcase and flipped the pages to Southeast U.S. He picked up the receiver. "You still there?"

"Yes I am."

"Great. Okay, let's pick a number for Waycross, Georgia. Can it have a couple zeros?"

"Sure, how about 912-555-2200?"

"Perfect." Brett said, and charged the fifty-nine ninety-five on his American Express.

"If you have email I can send you a receipt and directions for use of the voicemail."

"That'll work," Brett said, and gave her his address.

Brett had a small digital recorder and brought it with him to the office the following morning. He signaled Janet, one of the dental assistants, to come into his private office. "Hey Janet, you're from Savannah or somewhere in the south, aren't you?"

She batted her eyelashes together a couple times and said in an overdone drawl, "Well, shame on you Docta Raven. A cute northern boy like you should know this southern girl is from Atlanta."

Brett broke up laughing. "Janet, don't lose that accent, I want you to record a message on this machine for me."

She was very good. Again with a deep southern accent, Janet read the message into the recorder. "Hi there, y'all reached Dixie Aircraft Sales in Waycross Georgia. We're out of the office right now; however, if y'all leave us your name, number and reason for your call, we'll get right back. Bye now."

Brett clicked off the recorder. "Thanks, Janet; I'll nominate you for an academy award."

She batted her eyelashes again and said, "Y'all welcome," and hustled back to work.

Brett dialed his new number in Waycross Georgia and followed the directions to record an answer message. He played the recording of Janet into the machine and then played it back. He smiled as the answer message began, "Hi there. y'all reached Dixie Aircraft Sales…"

Brett retrieved the phone number for the Southeast AeroTrader and dialed it up.

After being put on hold for five minutes, a young lady connected. "Sorry for the wait, I can help you place the ad. What make and model?"

"It's a Beech Baron 58."

"Okay, so we'll list it under light twins?"

"That would be perfect."

"Okay, speak slowly and read me the ad."

Brett put the notepad next to the phone and read the text. "1992 Beech Baron 58, original owner, only 528 hours of total time, tan and blue exterior, tan leather interior, full King Avionics, Century-four autopilot, weather radar, de-ice boots and props. The owner wants this plane to go to an experienced Baron pilot. First $255 thousand takes it. 1-912-555-2200."

The woman read the ad back to him and paused near the end. "Are you sure the price is $255 thousand? That's about $150 thousand less than all the others in that age bracket."

"Yes, $255 thousand."

"Okay, it'll be in the next issue which will be out in five days."

"Great," Brett said, and gave her his credit card information.

CHAPTER 7

Brett was planning way ahead; he set up a meeting with Enrique and Manny. On the way down to Enrique's office in Redwood City, Brett gave Annie a quick background of the men she was about to meet.

Enrique was a small time gangster and a patient of Brett's. Brett liked him. After Brett had discovered that J.T. was somehow involved with black marketeers in Mexico, he needed Enrique's help. While trying to gather evidence relating to the crash of J.T.'s plane, Brett stumbled on the illegal movement of human organs from Mexico to the U.S. and had gotten beaten up pretty badly for sticking his nose into their business. When Brett needed to make a return trip, he asked Enrique for a bodyguard.

Enrique had given Brett his pick of the litter. Brett chose Manny, a guy in his thirties with an easy manner and a soft smile, and no physical resemblance to the gangster stereotype. He turned out to be a wise choice. Manny did his job well and provided the muscle which allowed them to make a midnight escape from a little Baja runway in Brett's rented plane. When they had parted at the airport in San Carlos, Manny had given him a hug and said, "If you ever need help again, I want ya to call me." Going into battle together had created a strong bond between them and now Brett was going to ask both him and Enrique to become partners in a plan to recover $5.5 million dollars of insurance money which was paid to J.T. Talbot's new wife after he had taken on the identity of Tony Russo. J.T. had faked the death of both men when he crashed the plane in Baja, Mexico.

Brett crossed the railroad tracks in Redwood City, drove up a broken down street, and pulled up in front of a small bar. Annie looked around in disbelief. "Holy shit, Brett, is this his office? It doesn't look safe to get out of the car."

Brett parked his new jade green Lexus SC400 coupe in front of the door that displayed a blinking sign overhead that read OPEN. "I know you won't believe it, but we're safer here than in our own neighborhood. No one would dare touch any of Enrique's friends or their possessions. In this neighborhood he's the equivalent of The Godfather."

Annie shot him a skeptical look and said, "It's your car."

They were greeted by a huge doorman who looked as if he had just escaped from San Quentin. He had tattoos up and down his beefy arms and a nasty scar that stretched from the corner of his left eye to his ear. "Enrique here? He's expecting me," Brett said.

A deep voice that sounded lower than baritone said, "You the jawbreaker?"

Brett thrust out his hand. "Yeah, Brett Raven. This is Annie."

A big smile transformed the scary face. "Good to meet ya, doc. I'm Omar. Nice to meet ya, ma'am." Omar pointed to a booth in the rear of the bar which Brett recognized as Enrique's private office.

As Brett and Annie approached the booth, two men jumped out to stand for the lady. Enrique was in his fifties, olive skin, brown eyes and extremely handsome. Manny hadn't changed and his baby face and cute smile made him look as if he had just walked out of a travel ad for Latin America.

Brett spoke first. "Enrique, Manny, this is Annie."

Enrique took both her hands in his. "Bienviendo, welcome, welcome."

Manny was next and shook hands with Annie.

"You're even more beautiful than Brett described."

Annie blushed and said, "It's great to meet you guys. Thanks for being such good friends to Brett."

Everybody slid into the booth. "What will it be? Beer, Margarita, Wine?" Enrique inquired.

It was only eleven in the morning; Both Brett and Annie opted for Pacificos.

Everybody made small talk until the beers were on the table. Then Enrique said, "Let's hear it. You said you had a proposition for us."

Brett took a swallow of the beer and said, "How would you guys like to make yourselves three or four hundred thousand dollars?"

The smiles disappeared. This was big money, even for Enrique. He lit a cigarette and said, "Doc, you goin' rogue? It must be illegal or you wouldn't be here."

"I really wouldn't say it's illegal, but I know that's an issue you don't usually worry too much about. We're going to steal money that was already stolen, and then we're going to return it to its original owner."

Manny was bewildered. "If we steal money and give it back to its original owner, how do we come out with anything?"

"It's called a recovery fee. Do the math, ten percent of $10.5 million."

Enrique snapped his fingers and a guy appeared at the table. "Get us a bottle of Patron. I don't care if it's only eleven o'clock; I think we're goin' to need somethin' stronger than beer."

Flight of Deception

The bottle of Tequila, along with four shot glasses, a salt shaker and a plate with lime wedges, miraculously appeared on the table. Enrique filled the glasses and pushed one in front of his three companions. He licked the skin between his left thumb and forefinger dropping a hefty portion of salt on the area. Then he licked the salt, threw the entire shot of Tequila down his throat and finished up by squeezing the lime between his teeth. Everyone followed his lead except Brett. He still had a cast on his left hand and had to handle the entire maneuver with only his right.

All eight eyes were glistening when Brett outlined the deal. "The insurance companies paid Annie $5 million dollars for the death of J.T. They paid me $190 thousand for the loss of my plane. They paid Maria Russo $4.25 million for the death of her husband Tony and also paid her a wrongful death claim for $1.25 million. Turns out I discovered that neither of those guys died in that plane crash. Worse yet, J.T. left his wife, Annie here, believing he was dead when he had actually had become Tony Russo and married Maria."

Manny looked perplexed. "I don't get it. If you have $5.2 million dollars, why go through all this to only end up with $1 million?"

Annie chimed in. "Manny, we don't want that money, it was all a scam. It would only be a matter of time anyway, before someone other than Brett figured it out. Then we would become accomplices and probably looking at jail time"

Enrique scratched his scalp. "What do you actually get out of this deal if you split the million with us?"

"We break even," Brett said. "Here's the story. J.T. was our best friend and airplane partner. After Annie and I split up, J.T. preyed on Annie and married her. Then he essentially ran off and married another woman leaving his bills behind. Annie's out $200 thousand for the bills and I'm out $200 thousand for a wrecked airplane. It's going to cost us about $200 thousand to set up the plan to recover the insurance money. That will leave at least four hundred thousand for your services."

Manny jumped in. "What if the plan doesn't work? What do we get out of it?"

"A couple months' vacation with all expenses paid," Brett replied.

Enrique wasn't buying it. "Come on, doc. You're setting this whole thing up and risking 200K just to break even?"

Brett smiled, he knew Enrique was smart. "In your business you understand the term payback. It's not the money for us. Yeah, it will be nice to get our money back and break even, but it's deeper than that; J.T. betrayed both of us. We want him to know there's a price for his betrayal."

Enrique nodded in agreement. "What are we going to have to do to earn our share?" He inquired.

"First of all, I know you're married; Manny are you?"

Manny looked surprised. "No, but I have a

girlfriend, is that a problem?"

Brett laughed, "Not at all, but I'd like you both to bring a lady along. I assume Enrique will bring his wife and you'll bring your girlfriend. If they agree, they'll play a part in the plan."

Enrique still didn't have an answer to his question. "Okay, so we agree to get involved and we bring along the gals. What exactly is this plan you keep referring to?"

"It's still a work in progress. When I have all the pieces together, we'll have a meeting and I'll lay it out. I guarantee you won't have to beat anyone up or kill anyone. This time you'll have to rely on your brains, and I know you guys have good ones."

Enrique was silent. Manny didn't say a word, knowing that it wouldn't be his decision; whatever Enrique decided would be decided for both of them. Enrique tapped his right index finger up and down on the table as Brett, Annie, and Manny watched him intently. Finally Enrique splashed another round of liquor into the shot glasses, licked his skin, added the salt, and downed the shot. The others did the same.

"To a profitable partnership," Enrique said.

"To a profitable partnership," The others said, as they placed the limes between their teeth.

CHAPTER 8

Brett and Annie were having breakfast at First Watch, a crowded Sunday morning spot in San Mateo. "I got the phone number and placed the ad," Brett said.

Annie looked up from her Chronicle. "When do you start checking the voicemails?"

"The AeroTrader should be out the day after tomorrow, we'll start then."

"What happens if he doesn't see it or doesn't take the bait?"

Brett made way for the pancakes that were being set down in front of him. "Let's think positively, I really feel we're in the right place. I'm going to need your help listening to the messages"

"Sure, but why?"

"I barely talked to J.T. in the last five years. You'll be able to recognize his voice better than I."

"I'll be glad to finger that bigamist."

Brett laughed, "Don't let your emotions in; they'll screw up your decision making."

Annie finished up her coffee. "I know; it's just hard to accept the fact that he was married to me and another person at the same time."

"Speaking of that, what did the divorce lawyer say?"

"I meant to tell you last night, but my hormones got in the way. Believe it or not, I'm getting an annulment. Otherwise, we'd have to prove to a judge that he's still alive."

"That's great, how long will it take?"

"About three months. I paid him the retainer already."

Brett leaned over the table and touched his hand to Annie's cheek. "That mean you'll think about marrying me?"

"Brett, I'm still afraid the past will haunt us. I have to get my head clear for myself. The recipe looks pretty good right now; let's not add an unknown ingredient."

He looked disappointed, "Okay, I promised I wouldn't pressure you. Just know I love you very much."

She reached over and stroked his hand, "I know and I love you too, but let's leave it where it is, okay?"

Brett tried to force a smile, but it looked like his

face was frozen. "Sure," he replied.

Wednesday evening Brett dialed the number he had set up in Waycross, Georgia. He hit *99 which allowed him access to the voicemail. It was empty.

Thursday he had one response to his ad. It was a young kid. "Hey man, I'm really interested in the Baron, give me a call. I'm in South Carolina, 843-555-6723." He called the number back and left a message that the plane had been sold.

The responses began to increase every day. He and Annie would listen to each one trying to pick up a voice that sounded familiar, but an entire week went by without any luck.

On the evening of day ten, as they were clicking through the voicemails, suddenly Annie turned pale and felt a chill run up her back. "Replay, replay that one," she stammered.

Brett tapped #11 jumping the messages backward. "Hi, I'm interested in the Baron. How come so cheap? Give me a call, 777-555-7752."

"Play it again," Annie said.

Brett backed it up again. "Hi, I'm interested in the Baron. How come so cheap? Give me a call, 777-555-7752."

Annie's eyes teared up. "You told me he was alive. I knew he was alive, but it wasn't real until just now. To me, that's a voice from the dead."

Brett backed it up one more time. "You sure, I

don't quite hear it."

"It's him, I'm sure of it," Annie said, while biting her lower lip.

Brett waited until Janet had a break from the treatment room and motioned her into his private office. "What's up?" she asked.

He handed her a piece of paper with a phone number and a script written on it. "I need another favor. I'm going to connect with a number in Georgia. I'd like you to use it and call this 777 number. If a guy answers, put on the southern charm and paraphrase this script."

Janet looked at the script. "No problem," she said.

Brett hooked up with his Georgia relay number and handed the phone to Janet. She dialed 777-555-7752 as Brett picked up the extension. A male voice answered.

"Hi, this is Candy from Dixie Aviation up here in Waycross. How y'all doin' today?"

There was a pause on the other end and then obviously recognition. "Oh yeah, you're the outfit with the Baron."

"That's right, Mr. Gillespie asked me to call ya. He's really sorry, but the Baron was sold the first day."

"I didn't figure it would last long at that price."

"He wanted me to tell you that he's pretty

sure he'll have another one coming in next month. Would you like a call?"

"Sure, you have my number."

"Who should Mr. Gillespie ask for?"

"Antonio, Antonio Russ."

"Great, I'll tell him, bye."

Brett kissed her on the cheek. "That was great. Remind me to tell the boss you should have a raise."

"But you're the boss."

Brett scratched his head. "Oh yeah, I almost forgot."

CHAPTER 9

Brett was heading out the door when Annie let it drop, "Brett, we have to talk."

Brett's radar was on high beam. "Oh, oh, this sounds serious. Should we talk now? I can be late checking in at the office."

"No, go ahead, I didn't mean to upset you. How about we meet for lunch, it'll wait till then."

"You sure?"

"Really," Annie replied. "Go ahead. I'll get a table at Pete's Harbor around eleven-thirty."

Brett wiped a bead of sweat from his upper lip. It always made him nervous when Annie's voice carried this tone. "Okay, eleven-thirty."

Brett tried to sneak by Ginger on his way from

the business office to his own, but she looked up and caught him in the act. "Why so quiet? If I didn't know better, I'd guess you were trying to avoid me."

He tried to smile but he was still worried about Annie's sudden request for a meeting. "Oh, it's not you, Ginger, I'm a little worried about Annie."

"I can grab two coffees and meet you in your back office. Let's talk about it."

Brett thought for a minute. Ginger was always someone he could talk to and she never betrayed his trust. "Sure, just sweetener in mine."

Ginger entered without knocking, set Brett's mug on his desk, and pulled up the recliner Brett used for cat naps. "So, what's brewing besides the coffee?"

Brett took a drink from the mug and fanned his mouth, "Oh, this is hot."

"It's coffee, what did you expect?"

"Feels like you heated it in the autoclave."

Ginger laughed, "I think you're stalling. Come on, talk."

"Annie's not real happy. She puts on an act, but I know she's pretty troubled. Finding out J.T. was alive and had disappeared with another woman was pretty deflating to her ego, even though she says she wasn't really in love with him."

"Have you talked to her about it?"

"Sure, but it's a demon I can't exorcise for her. Sometimes I wake up in the middle of the night and she's downstairs just walking around. I know it's eating at her."

Ginger nodded apologetically, "How about you guys? How's your relationship?"

"I wish I knew. We have no problems with the physical side, but I just wonder sometimes if I can meet her emotional needs. I'm trying real hard, but it's difficult for me to face some of our past straight on."

"Like what?"

"I never told you, but when Annie and I were in college, I forced her to have an abortion."

Ginger looked puzzled, "What do you mean, forced?"

"Well force is the wrong word, I coerced her; I just didn't give her much choice. That's really what caused us to divorce back in 1995. When she got pregnant again and had the miscarriage, we found out that another pregnancy could kill her and she would never have children; her anger was uncontrollable and she couldn't stand the sight of me."

Ginger got up and put a hand on Brett's shoulder. "Brett that was a long time ago, she must have forgiven you or she wouldn't have returned to live with you."

Brett's eyes misted over. "She says she's forgiven me, but can someone ever forgive a thing like that?"

Ginger was silent. She knew Brett always portrayed a wall of strength and for him to expose this vulnerable side wasn't easy. Then she asked, "Have you ever come to grips with it?"

He pulled a Kleenex from an open box and blew his nose. "In all honesty, no! I try to pretend I have, but I don't think I ever will."

"Do you think Annie wants to talk about it some more?"

"We're going to lunch today. Something is comin' my way and I'm scared shitless she's going to tell me she wants to leave me."

Ginger sat back down in the recliner. "Brett, maybe your guilt is causing you to over react. Is there anything else that might be bothering her?"

Brett sighed, "Where do I start? She needs something to do: Something to make her life meaningful: Something to get her out of bed in the morning."

"God, Brett, she's an intelligent, capable, attractive woman. She has a teaching credential, she worked here at the office and she's had a good job at Nordstrom. Surely she could go back to one of those."

He had a hang dog look. "I may have complicated that for her."

"What do you mean?'

"I'm going after J.T. She wants to help."

Ginger turned pale. "I thought you were through with that. Almost getting yourself killed by gangsters in Mexico didn't teach you a lesson?"

"This isn't going to be dangerous, just expensive."

"Why?"

"I want to get even with that son of a bitch."

"Does Annie?"

Brett reflected for a moment. "She says she does, but if I'm honest with myself, I have to admit it's all about me. I think Annie may actually be able to let go a lot easier than I can."

The intercom buzzed and a female voice came over it, "Hi Dr. Raven, is Ginger with you? There's an unhappy patient up here and I'm afraid she's going to have to settle him down."

"She'll be right there," Brett replied, and clicked off the intercom.

"Thanks Ginger, I'll keep you in the loop."

"Make sure you do," she said, as she scurried out the door.

Pete's Harbor is actually a pier in Redwood City with access to the San Francisco Bay; it houses several dozen slips filled with boats, many of which are permanent homes to their owners. There's also a little restaurant on the pier which could aptly be characterized as a 'dive' and it shares the same name as the pier, 'Pete's Harbor'.

Brett pulled his coupe into a self-made parking spot off the road on the edge of the dirt.

He knew Annie was already there. She had parked her SUV on the asphalt right next to the entrance.

Even though it was November, the sun was out and the temperature was almost seventy. Annie had found a table on the outside deck under a moth eaten umbrella and she was in the process of wiping the stained wooden table with a napkin as Brett sat down next to her.

"Hi," Brett said, as he reached over and gave her a kiss on the cheek.

"Hi," she responded, "You snuck up on me, anything new at the office?"

"Not really, everybody working except me."

"Relax, Brett, you'll be back there in a couple months."

"I know, just feeling sorry for myself. Did you get a menu?"

"Do we need one? Nothing's changed."

A waitress approached with two glasses of water. "Menus?" she asked.

"No, we're ready," Brett replied. He nodded toward Annie, "Go ahead."

Annie took a glass from the young girl and set it near her. "Burger, medium rare with Pepperjack and hold the fries; I'll have the salad with ranch."

Brett took his turn, "The same, only I'll take the fries. Oh yeah, and two Pale Ales."

The waitress retreated to the kitchen and there was silence. Finally Brett said, "So?"

"So what?" Annie replied.

"Was I mistaken, or were you upset this morning?"

Annie was hesitant to start. "Brett, are we getting in over our heads?"

"You mean with the insurance companies?"

"Everything: The insurance companies, J.T., Biff, Enrique, Manny, the legal system."

The waitress placed two beer mugs with the amber liquid in front of them. Brett acknowledged and waited for her to go to another table. "I don't think so, what do you think?"

"How 'bout the money. It's going to cost at least two hundred thousand dollars. If we can't touch the insurance money, where are you going to get it?"

"I have seven hundred and fifty thousand in my retirement plan. I can borrow what we need from there, and when we get our reward, I'll pay it back."

"What if your plan doesn't work? What then?"

The waitress was back with two red plastic baskets lined with paper and overflowing with juice from the hamburger meat. Brett and Annie passed the ketchup and mustard between them and then Brett said, "If it doesn't work, I guess I'll have to retire ten years later than I planned." They ate in silence until he broke the spell. "Do you want to just can the whole idea?"

"Brett, this is your deal and your money. I've already told you, if you need to do this, then do it; I'm not going to stand in your way."

"I need to do this, Annie, I really do."

"Okay, I won't bring it up again."

Silence hung over the table like a shroud on a coffin. Annie lightened the air, "This place is a dump but the burgers are the best."

Brett smiled, "Yeah, the best." He gnawed away at the sandwich until finally he had the nerve to bring up the subject. "Annie, what's the real reason you wanted to talk today?"

Annie put down her sandwich and it was obvious to Brett she was carefully organizing her thoughts. "Brett, you know I'm having problems dealing with what has taken place in the past and with what's in store for my future."

"I know. Ever since our talk in San Francisco, I've tried leave you alone and not be your problem solver."

She reached over and patted his hand. "I really appreciate that. It's given me the freedom to work things out in my head."

He didn't want to ask the next question for fear of the answer, but he did anyway, "Have you come to any conclusions?"

Annie could see the sweat form above Brett's upper lip. "Brett, don't worry; I'm not packing my suitcase."

Brett gave a smile and wiped his upper lip with one of the checkered napkins piled at the end of the table. "That's a relief; I thought you were going to leave me."

"Brett, I want us to have a life together. Remember, I told you my problems are about me, not about you. Living without you won't solve them. I have to decide what I'm going to do with the rest of my life. I have to decide how to feel good about myself and how to leave a footprint, no matter how small, that will remain after I leave this earth."

"Sounds like you've made some decisions."

"I quit teaching fifteen years ago to help you

start your practice. I loved teaching, I loved the kids, and I loved the feeling of self-worth it gave me." She smiled. "I'm going back to it."

"That's great. When will you start?"

"I'm thinking in about six years."

Brett's eyes opened wide. "Six years? Why so long?"

"I'd like to have a baby first, and I'd like you to have it with me."

"Annie, I want a child too, but you know as well as I, that we can't take a chance with your life in order to create another."

"I've found a way. Ever hear of a surrogate?"

"A what?"

"A woman who carries a baby for someone else. She's called a surrogate."

Brett looked incredulous. "How does that work? Would the surrogate be the mother and I be father?"

"I'm sure that's one way, but that's not what I'm talking about. I read up on it. There's such a thing as gestational surrogacy where we can use my egg and your sperm. The child would be our child."

Brett looked perplexed. "How exactly can that happen?"

"Apparently there are specialty doctors who create an embryo in the laboratory with the mother's egg and the father's sperm and then they implant it into the surrogate's uterus. She carries the baby to term."

"Why would she want to do that?"

"I'm sure there can be a bunch of reasons: altruism, vanity, money. Maybe all three."

Brett's mind was spinning. A child, their own child, could it really happen? "Who picks the surrogate?"

"From what I read, we do. There're agencies that solicit them, and the future parents interview and get to know them before making a decision. Legal documents are signed to guarantee the parents will get the baby in case the surrogate changes her mind half way through."

Brett sat silently, processing the information. "I'm sorry," Annie said. "You probably feel like I dropped a bomb on you. It's just that I really want a child and I want to have it with you. Don't make up your mind right now. Think about it and we'll discuss it more later."

Brett nodded and left a twenty dollar bill on the table. "My car is near yours. Let's go home and figure this out."

CHAPTER 10

Both cars pulled into the garage at the same time. Brett followed Annie into the living room and Annie spoke first, "Brett, I sense you have some trepidation. I don't want to pressure you and I don't want to make this a condition for our relationship, but I want you to know this is something I need."

"You're reading me wrong. I don't have any reservations about it. I was just thinking how I've always felt I could never make up for my actions twenty years ago, and now you're giving me a chance to do it. I'm overwhelmed, I'm happy, and I want to do it."

"You sure?"

"Never more sure of anything."

Annie came over and put her arms around his neck. "I'd give you a kiss but you have sweat all over your face. Go take a shower."

Brett was in the shower. There was no door; just a tiled entry wall to walk around and he had his back to the opening. He put his head under the rushing spray and at the same time felt the warmth of dry skin against his back. Annie slipped her arms around to his front, her raised nipples caressing his back as she kissed the nape of his neck. Brett didn't move or speak.

Annie moved in closer straddling his right leg with both of hers. Brett instinctively began to move his leg against her groin. Annie's hands which were clasped together at Brett's waist, slowly inched lower until they eased through his pubic hair and gently grasped him as he became hard.

Brett began to speak but Annie stopped him. "Shh, don't say anything, just close your eyes."

Brett did what he was told. Annie began to move her right hand up and down between his legs while her left one gently caressed from below. Brett felt the tension rise and leaned against the tile wall with both hands as the water drenched their bodies. Suddenly he couldn't hold back and Annie felt the warmth of his eruption flow onto her hand. Brett turned around and pulled Annie close. He kissed her hard and forced his tongue between her lips. She kissed him back and put her arms around his neck as she pushed her belly against his.

The water was still pouring down over their bodies as Brett reached for the bar of soap. He put it in his right hand and started to lather Annie's back with it. When his hand was filled with the froth from the soap, he dropped it to the floor and let his hand slide down between the cleavage of her buttocks. He kept working his hand between them until his middle finger could feel the opening. Carefully he caressed the orifice until he could feel her breathing heavily. He withdrew his finger and let it slip forward between her already lubricated lips; finding the erect skin just above them, he gently rubbed in a circular motion. Annie began to pant and as she reached a climax, she dug her nails into Brett's back.

Brett reached for the controls and turned off the water. They stepped out of the shower and grabbed towels as Annie looked at both of them in the mirror. What a contrast; He was almost six feet, she was barely five. Brett's skin was dark, hers was light. He had black hair and deep brown eyes; she had light hair and green eyes. She couldn't help but think, "What a beautiful baby we can make."

Instead of using it on himself, Brett took his towel and began to dry Annie. He did it slowly and methodically. As he reached between her legs he began to rub the same area he had chosen in the shower. Annie responded quickly and put her arms around his neck and planted a deep kiss.

The bathroom was carpeted and Brett eased Annie down on it. He lay over her and caressed her breasts with his right hand, while teasing her erect nipples. Annie could feel Brett's new arousal rubbing against her thigh and she maneuvered her legs into a spread eagle position. He propped up on his elbows and guided himself between them.

Annie raised her feet behind Brett's back, crossed her ankles, and squeezed. He was sucked in as deep as he could go. Annie slowly let go and Brett began to withdraw, only to have her squeeze again, drawing him back in. Brett moved to her lead and just like a slow dance they fell into rhythm.

The cadence went up tempo and soon they were slamming against each other. Brett was trying desperately to hold back until he could wait no longer. Just as he released, Annie screamed out and their sweating bodies relaxed against each other.

They lay silent for ten minutes until Annie finally broke it, "Let's start looking for names." She whispered.

After dinner Annie and Brett got into bed early. "You are serious about this aren't you? Annie asked.

"Absolutely," Brett replied. "How do we go about it?"

"The first step is to find a reliable agency. Why don't I contact my gynecologist and get a referral; but I want you to come with me to the agency."

Brett pulled her close and held her tight. "Annie, this is going to be our baby, we're doing this together, like all parents do."

"When are you headed for Florida?"

"I'd like to go down there in a day or two. The sooner we find him and get things in place, the sooner we'll be done with this nightmare."

"When should I schedule, after I get a referral to an agency?"

Brett thought for a moment, "Today is Monday, if I go to Florida on Wednesday, I'll be home by the end of the week. Make us an appointment for anytime next week."

"You sure now?"

"One hundred percent sure," he replied, as he smothered her with a kiss.

"I love you Brett."

"I love you too Annie."

CHAPTER 11

Annie pulled up in front of the United Terminal. Brett grabbed his overnight case from the back seat and leaned over to kiss her goodbye. "Call ya when I get there and hopefully see you in three or four days."

Annie gave him a return kiss, "Be careful."

"This is the easy part. The next trip will start the intrigue."

"Never know, keep your eyes open."

He kissed her again. "You know I will," he said, as he hopped out of the car and disappeared through the sliding glass doors into the terminal.

The five hour flight to Miami was non-stop and with the three hour time change got Brett in at three in the afternoon. He went directly to the Avis counter and rented one of the newly released Cadillac Escalades.

While waiting for the car to be delivered to the rental office building, Brett thumbed through the yellow pages of the Miami phone book searching the section titled Investigators. An ad caught his eye.

Discreet Investigation Associates
We work for you and only you
252 Miami Parkway, Miami Fl.
Drake Caymen Lic. # 32602
305-555-5600

Brett pulled out his cell and dialed the number and a pleasant voice answered on the second ring. "We're discreet, may I help you?"

Brett smiled into the phone, "Yes I'd like to make an appointment with Mr. Caymen."

"Wonderful," the voice answered. "Could you come in this afternoon at four-thirty?"

Brett looked at his watch. "That would be great," he answered.

"Okay, we'll see you at in about an hour."

"Do you want my name?' Brett asked.

"Don't need it, remember we're discreet. See you at half past four. Bye." She hung up.

Brett parked the rental car about a block away and walked to Drake Caymen's office. It wasn't the stereotypical detective office tucked away on the second floor of an old building with an unmarked door and a frizzy haired secretary chewing gum and smoking cigarettes. It was very professional. The name on the door was simply <u>Discreet I.A.</u> and it opened into a reception room with new carpets, wicker chairs and artwork on the walls.

The receptionist was seated behind a modern desk and looked up when Brett walked in. He recognized the voice as the same one he had talked to earlier on the phone. "You must be our four-thirty visitor. My name's Veronica but everyone calls me Tootsie."

Brett returned the young lady's smile and replied, "Hi, Tootsie. Yes I talked to you earlier. My name's Br..."

She interrupted, "No need to give me your name, just have a seat; you don't need to fill out any forms either. Mr. Caymen will take down any personal information he needs. Coffee?"

"No thanks," Brett said, and flopped down into one of the wicker chairs. Before he could get into a thrilling story in People Magazine about a bisexual TV star who had just come out of the closet, Tootsie motioned him toward a private office, opened the door and led him in. This room was also very professional in appearance and gave the impression of an attorney's office, with a large oak desk and floor to ceiling bookcases.

A handsome guy popped out of his chair with a hand extended. Brett was taken back for a moment. The man had an uncanny resemblance to J.T. He was about six three, blue eyes, good build, and in his early fifties. The only feature which set them apart was his brown hair; J.T. was a blond. "Hello, I'm Drake Caymen."

The receptionist left the room closing the door behind her. Brett extended his right hand for a shake. "Brett Raven."

"Looks like a nasty accident to that left hand. Anything to do with this visit?"

Drake sat down behind his desk and motioned Brett into a chair facing him. "Sort of, but we won't get into that," Brett replied.

"Fair enough," Drake said. "Brett, I want as little personal information from you as possible. Most of my records are kept in my head. I don't like computer or paper trails which can come back to haunt me or my clients. We'll call each other by first names and any billing we'll do verbally. Anything I write down I'll show you after our appointments and if you desire will be shredded. How does that sound?"

"Very clandestine."

"Yeah, exactly. Our work together will be a secret between only you and me. Not even Tootsie will know."

"Sounds good," Brett said.

"Okay, let me know what you need and I'll tell you if I can help and how much it will cost."

Brett took a piece of paper out of his pants pocket and handed it to Drake. Written on it was the number 772-555-7752. "That phone number belongs to a guy who initially was known as J.T. Talbot. Last time I saw him he was going by the name Tony Russo, but he now may be using another alias, Antonio Russ. I need you to find out the address where he lives."

Drake studied the number. "Looks like the West Palm Beach area."

"That's what I figured also by looking through the phone directories."

"What do you want after I find his address?"

Brett thought it out for a minute. "He has a wife who was last known as Maria. I need to find out the actual name each is going by. In addition, I need to know their habits: where they go each day, where they eat out, where the wife shops and has her hair done... stuff like that."

"When do you need it?"

"Soon."

"The address and names will be easy. Tracking their habits will take time."

"How much time?"

Drake scratched his head. "At least two weeks after I find them."

"That will work, let's talk fees."

"Sure," Drake replied. "My hourly is $100 plus expenses. My associates are $50. I'm guessing with the surveillance, you're looking at about $7,500. We'll need $2,500 before we start, another $2,500 in a week, and the balance when we deliver the information."

Brett nodded approvingly, "No problem. I'll be

back in California so I'll give you the entire $7,500 tomorrow. If it goes longer with more fees, I'll send them to you."

"Some clients don't want to pay with checks or credit cards. What's your preference?"

Brett thought about it. "Now that you mention it, the fewer records the better. I'll go to the bank this afternoon and drop off cash in the morning. I trust you, no receipts necessary."

"That's fine. I'll need to get a hold of you in California. Give me a secure phone number I can reach you on."

Brett jotted down his cell number and handed it to Drake. "Thanks, Drake. If this goes well I may need additional help from you."

Drake came out from behind his desk and offered Brett his hand again. "I appreciate the confidence you've placed in me. I'll be in touch as soon as I have some reliable information."

Brett shook with Drake and said, "I'll be waiting. Tell Tootsie I'll drop off an envelope in the morning, good luck."

Brett turned around as he was leaving the office, "Hey Drake, I need an upscale shop for men's and women's clothes. Any suggestions?"

"If you're willing to drop some gold, I'd head for Dolce & Gabbana. Take Collins Avenue up the beach to Bal Harbor, it's just north of 96th street."

Brett found a motel on Biscayne Boulevard, not far from the clothier. After settling into his room he dialed the number of H. J. Hathaway Properties, a real estate firm in Palm Beach who handles pricey, exclusive properties. "Hathaway Properties, how may I direct your call?" a female voice said.

"I'm interested in renting a property for the winter. Any agents still there?"

"Patricia Delorean is here. Whom may I say is inquiring?"

"My name is Doctor Raven."

"Just a moment doctor, I'm putting you on hold for just a second."

A mature husky female voice picked up the line. "This is Patricia, how may I help you, Doctor Raven?"

"Hi, Patricia. I'm down in Miami and I'll be in Palm Beach tomorrow. I'm interested in leasing an estate for the winter and I was hoping you'd have a few places to show me."

"No problem, doctor, we have several really wonderful spots on the island. What time would be good for you?"

"I'll be out of here by noon, how 'bout two o'clock?"

Brett could tell she was smiling. "Wonderful, do you know how to find us?"

"Not really," he said, and Patricia detailed the directions to him.

CHAPTER 12

Brett was up early. After a shower and shave he checked out of the motel, grabbed some breakfast and located the nearest Bank of America; he was at a teller's window just after it opened at nine a.m. and handed her his debit card. "I've pre-arranged with my branch in California for large cash withdrawals. I need to withdraw seventy-five hundred."

The teller took his card and ID and went to check with the manager who looked up, gave Brett a once over glance, and put his initials on the withdrawal slip. The teller counted out seventy-five one hundred dollar bills and put them into a manila envelope. "Thank you Dr. Raven, enjoy your stay," she said.

"Thanks, I will," Brett responded, as he waved goodbye.

Brett dropped the manila envelope off with Tootsie and re-traced his route back toward Bal Harbour.

Drake was right; he was going to drop a few bucks shopping at Dolce & Gabbana. As Brett inspected the racks he noticed the suits started at $2,800 and went as high as $7,400; the least expensive sport coat went for $1,500. A good looking salesman approached as soon as he spotted Brett. He was perfectly dressed; a poster boy for the store. He either made a lot on commissions or got a fifty percent discount. Brett thought, probably both.

"And what can we help you with today?" The Gorgio Armani clone asked.

"I need a casual outfit; lightweight slacks and jacket and maybe a linen shirt."

"Very good," the man replied, sensing a sale in the making.

"One thing though, I need to wear them this morning." Brett replied.

"No problem sir. I'm guessing about a thirty-nine jacket and thirty-two, thirty-two on the pants."

Brett was impressed. "You nailed it." Brett decided on a pair of light tan rayon/silk slacks, a navy blue linen jacket, and a white silk shirt. At the last minute he opted for a pair of light brown casual loafers that could be worn without socks.

While the slacks were being cuffed, Brett had a cup of coffee with the salesman. They exchanged names and it turned out his wasn't Gorgio; it was Norman. "So Norm, how long you been with the store?"

Norman dropped the airs he had put on forty-five minutes earlier. "Actually, I just started. I really appreciate your sale; it will help my numbers the first week."

All of a sudden Brett started to like the guy. "Norm, I'll be back in about two months. You're going to do wardrobes for a couple guys and gals. I'm guessing with the prices here, we'll spend about 25K."

Norman's face lit up. "Oh Dr. Raven, I'd be so honored. Let me give me you my card, if you call ahead, I'll spend the entire day with your people."

Brett's pants came out at the same time as the card. He took the card and shook Norman's hand. "Mind if I put on the rags? I'm headed up to Palm Beach and have to look good."

"Absolutely, and thanks again. Don't forget to call me now."

"Don't worry, I won't forget." Brett changed clothes, put the $2,400 charge on his American Express and nodded goodbye to Norman.

CHAPTER 13

It took Brett an hour and twenty minutes to make the seventy mile drive from Miami to Palm Beach. Palm Beach is actually an island, with the Atlantic Ocean on the east, the Intracoastal Waterway on the west, and connection to the mainland via three bridges.

Brett crossed over to the island using the Flagler Memorial Bridge and found his way to Worth Street where Hathaway Properties was strategically located between Tiffany and Gucci. He parked the Escalade, grabbed his new linen jacket from the back seat, and slipped it on over his silk shirt.

Patricia was waiting in the reception area to

greet him. She was probably in her middle sixties, but was trying her hardest to look in her forties. Her hair was dyed platinum blonde and her skin was pulled a little tight from one too many facelifts. She kept her figure trim, but apparently had felt the need to enhance it with a thirty-six D boob job complete with a deep cleavage, which she displayed with the help of a low cut blouse.

As soon as Brett entered the opulent office, Patricia rushed toward him, hand extended. "Dr. Raven, it's so nice to meet you. How was the drive from Miami?"

He took her hand and replied, "Just fine, shorter than I thought."

She led him into her private office where the walls were covered with huge colored photographs of gorgeous homes and estates all taken with a backdrop of the Atlantic Ocean. "Are you hungry at all? I can have some snacks brought in."

"No thanks, maybe something to drink," Brett replied.

"Coffee, soft drink, wine?" Patricia asked.

"Just a diet coke would be great."

Patricia retrieved two cokes from the bar refrigerator, poured them into glasses with ice, gave one to Brett, and took one for herself. She motioned Brett to a leather chair in front of a coffee table and she took one facing him. "So Dr. Raven, I assume you're planning a vacation here in Florida. Where's home?"

"California. I want to bring my family and in-laws here for about three months this winter."

Patricia was an expert on sizing up her customers. The clothes Brett wore and the way he carried himself, indicated to her that he could afford what she had to offer. "How big a place are you looking for?"

Brett jiggled the ice cubes around in his glass and gave Patricia a wide smile, "I want an estate. My father in law made a fortune in the wine business. He just sold two wineries and this will be a long awaited getaway for him. His family is huge and we'll probably have family coming and going all winter."

Patricia smiled back trying not to stretch her skin too much. "I have just what you're looking for. There are three places available, all with ocean fronts. One is ten bedrooms, the other two are eight." She opened up a velvet covered scrapbook and slipped it in front of Brett. "Take a peek through these. The three I mentioned are on pages ten through eighteen."

Brett took the volume and leafed through it. All three properties were located on South Ocean Boulevard and were valued between fifteen and twenty million dollars. Brett picked one out and showed it to Patricia, "Any chance we could look at this one along with the other two?"

"We can get into the one you picked out, but the owners are in the other two right now so we can only drive by them."

"That would be fine," Brett replied.

Patricia scooped up a ring of keys and led the way to the parking lot. She pointed to a silver Mercedes SL500 convertible and popped the electronic door opener. Brett opened the driver's door for her and then took a seat on the passenger side. The engine roared to life and Patricia left a small patch of rubber on the blacktop as she headed for South Ocean Boulevard.

In less than ten minutes the Mercedes pulled up in front of a property fenced off by black wrought iron. Patricia punched in four numbers on a metal keyboard and the set of double gates opened for them.

While the Mercedes slowly negotiated the hundred yard circular driveway, Brett took in the view of the sprawling grounds with their manicured grasses and plethora of Palm trees. Patricia pulled to a stop in front of the main residence. It looked like the entrance to a hotel; finished in smooth white stucco with terra cotta roof tiling and multiple paned windows separated by Teak moldings. The exterior entry was done in three foot granite squares with two story high balustrades on each side of the front doors.

Patricia again entered four numbers into a keypad adjacent to the entry and one of the front doors clicked open. Although the outside of the house looked a bit ostentatious, the inside was tastefully done. The flooring was a combination of stone and hardwoods with area rugs in every room. The furniture had a tropical flair, using rattan, wicker and overstuffed cushions. The living area, master bedroom and kitchen all faced east, with a view of the pool, beach and Atlantic Ocean. There were six bedrooms and seven bathrooms in the main house and another two bedrooms and two baths in the guest cottage, which was detached from the main house and faced the pool from the north side of the property. On the south side of the property was a pool house with one bedroom and its own bath, and near the ocean was a beach house with another bedroom and bath.

Brett nonchalantly asked, "What would this house run me?"

Patricia opened a binder she had brought with her and thumbed through it until she found the address of the house. "Here it is. A three month minimum is required at $29,500 a month. The utilities and gardening are included, but housekeeping is separate at $400 a week. There's also a $10,000 security deposit."

Brett looked unfazed. "Could I get it for January, February and March?"

Patricia was delighted. "I'll check, but it looks like no problem. Do you want to drive by the other two?"

"I'd like to if it's not too much trouble. Do they run about the same?"

"Within a thousand a month," Patricia replied.

The other two properties were equally impressive from the road and Brett assumed they would serve him just as well as the first.

Back in Patricia's office, Brett took out a small notebook and a pen. "I want to get this down. For the three months I'd give you a check for ninety-eight five which includes the refundable deposit and we'd pay the housekeeper as we use her."

"Exactly."

Brett continued to write in his notebook, "Could you give me the three addresses so I don't mix them up in my mind?"

Patricia went to the Xerox machine and ran off three copies. "Here's the cover page for each property. The picture will remind you which is which."

Brett got up to leave, "Thanks, Patricia, I really like the one you showed me. I'll get back to you and we can precise the dates and the fees."

She thrust out her hand, "Thank you, Doctor Raven, I'll look forward to your call."

CHAPTER 14

The next day Brett checked out early from his West Palm Beach motel. He had two more important agenda items.

The county recorder for Palm Beach County is located in West Palm on North Dixie Highway. Brett arrived there at eight fifty and only had to wait ten minutes for it to open. A petite woman in her early sixties with gray hair and horned rim glasses was the first clerk to arrive. "What can I help you with?" she asked Brett.

"I'm looking at three properties on the island. Could you give me the public information on them?"

"Probably, do you have the parcel numbers?"

Oh, oh, Brett thought. "I don't have the parcels

but I have the addresses."

Very officiously the little lady said, "You'll have to look up the parcel numbers in the cross reference address listings."

Brett noted the name tag on the lady's blouse. He flashed his wide smile and placed his right hand on hers. "Mazie, my name is Brett. I'm not from around here and I have a plane to catch back to California in two hours. Any way you could kind of help me get the parcel numbers?"

Mazie's cheeks started to show a little pink as she took in Brett's smile. "Maybe this once, but don't tell anyone."

"I can keep a secret, thanks Mazie." Brett said, as he handed her the addresses of the three homes on South Ocean Boulevard.

The little lady scurried off and returned ten minutes later with three parcel numbers and a moldy smelling green canvas covered volume about eighteen inches square and six inches thick. "Brett, you can use the cubicle in the corner. Good luck."

Brett nestled into the cubicle and began sifting through the record book. He found each parcel and jotted down the information he needed.

PARCEL #001-238-6994
Owner: Dehavilland Family Trust
Appraisal 1998: $16,200,000
Mortgage Holder: None

PARCEL #010-877-2400
Owner: Carlos Alberto Rojas
Appraisal 1996: $17,650,000
Mortgage Holder: None

PARCEL #099-131-6740
Owner: Ruth Clement & Otto Clement
Appraisal 1989: $17,400,000
Mortgage Holder: Bank of America, $4,500,000

Brett closed the book and a puff of dust rose from it. He brought it back to the desk and leaned over giving the custodian a peck on the cheek. "Thanks, Mazie. You're the best."

She blushed again and said, "Glad to help, Brett. Have a good trip home."

Brett sat in his car and fumbled through his papers until he found Patricia Delorean's personal phone number. He used his cell and gave it a call. She quickly picked up, "Patricia here."

"Hi, Patricia, this is Brett Raven. I'll take the one you showed me, starting January 1st."

"Wonderful, any questions on the terms?"

"No; if you can draw up the contract, I'll sign it and leave you a check before I catch my plane this evening."

"I'll have everything ready. See you about five?"

"See you at five," Brett said, and hung up.

Brett had gone through the yellow pages at the motel the night before and had written down the address of what appeared to be a large commercial real estate firm in West Palm Beach, J. Granville & Associates. A well-dressed receptionist greeted him and escorted him into Frank Reynolds's office.

"What can I do for you, Brett?" Frank asked, after being introduced by the receptionist.

"I need a small office for a couple months."

Frank rubbed his chin, "That's a tough one; most of our leases are a year minimum. How big does it have to be?"

"Actually, small is good."

"Hey, I may have something. Ever hear of a condominium executive suite?"

Brett admitted he never had.

"Here's how it works. The suite takes up the entire floor in a very nice building. There's a common reception room with a receptionist and each business rents a private office within the master suite. Clients are directed from the common reception area to each individual office. The receptionist answers your phone line with your greeting and relays the call or the message to you. As an added perk there's a conference room which can be reserved in advance. It gives the impression of a large business structure, but in actuality, it's a bunch of small ones."

Brett was interested, "How long a lease?"

"We just had a business move out. I can let you have the office, furnished or not, four hundred square feet, for three months until we get a permanent client."

"How much?"

Frank jotted a group of figures on his notepad. "How about five dollars a foot for the office and a flat five hundred for the receptionist, reception room, and conference room. Total of twenty-five hundred a month."

Brett was ecstatic. "Can I see it?"

"Let's go,"

The suite was even nicer than Frank had described. It was on the sixth floor of the Florida National Bank Building and was occupied by six other companies, all involved in finance of one sort or another. It was perfect. "I'll take it. Can we wait till January to occupy?"

"No problem," Frank replied. "Let's fill out the paperwork."

CHAPTER 15

Annie was double parked outside the terminal, keeping her eyes out for the cop who was monitoring traffic. Just as he started toward her, she spotted Brett emerging from the sliding glass doors. She gave a tap on the horn and he broke into a trot to reach her before the policeman. He threw his overnight case on the back seat and slammed the door shut at the same time as Annie popped the accelerator.

"How'd it go?" she asked.

"Perfect. Even better than I could have imagined."

"Did you commit all the money in your retirement fund?"

Brett chuckled, "Not quite, but a lot."

"Still time to change your mind," Annie said, as she merged into the southbound lane on highway 101.

"No, I'm committed both emotionally and financially."

"Did you get us a nice place to stay?" she asked.

"It ain't a Motel 6, believe me; I think you'll be pleasantly surprised."

"When do we go into phase two?"

"I still have a few more loose ends to tie up first. I'm planning on the second of January."

"What do you have left to set up?" she asked.

"Ever been in a private jet?"

Annie laughed, "Don't tell me you're buying one."

"I wish. No, I have a better idea. Get ready for a test ride."

Annie rolled her eyes, "Whatever."

"Tell me about the appointment at the institute," Brett said.

"It's set for two p.m. on Monday. It's up in the city, so we probably should have lunch up there first."

"I think we'll be too excited to eat."

"You're probably right; my stomach is doing flips right now."

Annie took the Holly Street off ramp and started up the hill to the townhouse as they both sat in silence. "What're you thinking?" Brett finally asked.

"I'm thinking how lucky I am that you waited for me so that we could have a second chance.

Brett leaned over and kissed her right cheek. I'm the lucky one," he said.

CHAPTER 16

LGTI was the logo engraved on the door of the Life's Greatest Treasure Institute located on the 14th floor of the 450 Sutter Building in San Francisco. Brett and Annie checked in with the receptionist and took a seat in the waiting area. As they perused the room they admired the walls which were painted light pink and light blue and were covered with black and white photos of children in cribs, schools, and on playgrounds.

Within ten minutes a woman in her early fifties approached and introduced herself. "Dr. and Mrs. Raven, I'm Liz; I'll be your counselor here at LGTI." They shook hands and she led them down the hall and into her office. There were two couches in the middle of the room separated by a coffee table. Brett and Annie took seats on one and Liz on the other.

"How did you find us?" Liz inquired.

"My ob/gyn referred us." Annie replied.

"Wonderful, that's where most of our referrals come from. You indicated in your application that you were interested in the Gestational Surrogacy Program."

"Is that the one where we use my egg and Brett's sperm?" Annie responded.

"Exactly; the doctors create an embryo in vitro, in other words outside the body, and then plant it into the uterus of our surrogate."

"How successful is the planting procedure?" Brett asked.

"That's a complicated question. I think you're asking what the live birth success rate is since that's your goal. Our figures show it to be around 45-55%."

Annie was getting excited but also nervous. "How does it work exactly?"

"Brett's part is easy since all he has to do is contribute sperm on the day we need it. Your part is a bit harder. You'll be given drugs to stimulate the production of eggs and when the time is right, the doctors will remove several of them from your ovaries."

"Is it painful?"

"It's a lot easier than passing a baby through a birth canal. The doctors introduce local anesthesia and whatever the discomfort level, every mother has said it was worth it."

Liz slowed the conversation; this was a lot for Annie and Brett to absorb. When she continued she said, "The eggs are fertilized in the laboratory and when embryos are produced, they are placed into the uterus of the surrogate."

"Did you say embryos plural?" Annie asked.

Liz gave a smile; the question was a routine one. "Yes, usually up to four embryos will be planted in the surrogate's uterus." She read the reaction on their faces. "I know the next question. What if all four embryos are successful? The answer is they rarely are; however, there's a good chance that more than one will plant itself, which means twins or triplets. You have to be prepared for that."

Silence pervaded the room until Brett asked, "What about the surrogate? Who do you get to do it and why do they do it?"

"Every one of our women is already a mother. They know the process, they love the process and they are willing to go through it again to pass on the joy of parenthood to others. Each of them is also handsomely rewarded. I think you know the process is expensive."

"How expensive?" Annie asked.

"It varies, but I'd count on between seventy and eighty thousand dollars."

Annie looked nervously at Brett. "I knew it was costly, how does the fee break down?" he asked.

Liz took a pair of brochures off the table and handed one to each of them. The fees are listed inside, and there are three big ones: the first is for our agency and it runs $19,000. The second is the fee to the surrogate, which is usually about $22,000. In addition, you'll pay the surrogate $200 a month for miscellaneous expenses such as gas, parking, meals, child care, and anything else that might come up. Also, there's a couple thousand dollars for maternity clothes and lost work days."

Annie was getting discouraged as she looked over the brochure, "What are these other fees that you have listed?"

"Those are attorney fees to draw up agreements which run $5,000, and also the other big one for medical costs, that can vary between $15,000 and $20,000."

"If we decide to go ahead, what's the next step?" Annie asked.

Liz handed them each another brochure. "This will cover what we talked about and more. The next step is a series of lab tests for both of you, and of course you'll have to interview and pick a surrogate here at our facility."

Annie and Brett got up, shook hands with Liz and assured her they would call within a few days. When they got back into the car Brett asked, "So, what do you think?"

"Oh Brett, it's exciting; I never dreamed this could happen. Can you handle the costs?"

"I can come up with the money, so it's not an issue"

She looked relieved, "It sounds like we better be prepared for at least two cribs."

He smiled. "That's just fine with me."

CHAPTER 17

Annie was tossing and turning; she just couldn't fall back asleep. She hated to take them, but she knew there was a bottle of Ambien in the medicine cabinet. Usually five milligrams would be enough to put her back to sleep for at least four hours. She looked at the clock; four a.m. If she got out of bed and took one now, she would sleep until at least eight.

She dragged herself to the bathroom and rummaged through the medicine cabinet until she found the sleeping pills. Each tablet was ten milligrams, so she broke one in half and chugged it down with a glass of water. On her way back to bed she heard a strange noise in the front of the house.

It was Thursday night and the garbage cans had been put out for collection on Friday morning. There were two of them: one for food, one for recycle items. The noise seemed to be coming from the driveway where the cans were placed for pickup.

Their bedroom was on the second floor and had a window facing the front of the house. Annie quietly went to it, separated the curtains, and peeked out. She was startled. Someone was going through the recycle can, picking out paper items and stuffing them into a plastic garbage bag.

She went back to the bed and gently shook Brett. He awakened with a start. "Annie, what's wrong?"

"You won't believe this, but there's a familiar fat man going through our garbage."

Brett jumped out of bed and went to the window. Sure enough he could make out the features of Biff Erskine as he rummaged through the garbage.

"What's he looking for?" Annie asked.

"Probably anything we may have thrown out that would give him a hint as to where J.T. is or what our plan is."

"Is there anything to find?"

"I doubt it, we've been shredding everything."

Annie became indignant. "Let's go down there and confront the bastard. Maybe call the police."

Brett thought for a minute. "Let's not, I'm guessing this isn't the first time he's been here and probably not the last. We may be able to turn this to our advantage. Go back to sleep and we'll discuss it over coffee in the morning."

"I couldn't sleep before I saw him, how am I going to now?"

"Get back in bed and cuddle up with me. I won't go to sleep until you doze off."

The pill did its job and Annie stayed asleep until ten minutes to nine. Brett usually was out of the house by eight-thirty; however, this morning he hung around not wanting Annie to wake up to an empty house. She staggered down the stairs still feeling the effects of the Ambien.

Brett spotted her. "I was wondering if you were still alive. Coffee?"

"A big mug please."

Annie sat down at the breakfast bar and Brett fetched the coffee. He set a mug in front of Annie and brought another for himself. She took a big gulp and said, "What did you mean, 'turn this to our advantage?'"

"We have no way of knowing, but Biff may be getting close. He's not as dumb as he looks, perhaps we could steer him in the wrong direction."

Annie looked up from her coffee, "You mean plant something in our garbage?"

"Precisely," Brett answered.

"What did you have in mind?"

"I'm not sure yet, but I'll figure out something."

CHAPTER 18

Right after Brett had opened his dental practice in 1984, the Evans family, was referred to him. Their son, Rob was an atypical sixteen year old. He never talked to Brett about sports, girls, music or movies; instead he babbled nonstop about computers, algorithms, and ideas for startup companies.

Six years later, right out of Santa Clara University, he and two of his classmates convinced a venture capital firm in Silicon Valley to fund their startup company. The internet was emerging and Rob and his partners had a concept that would allow rapid navigation through it. The concept was soon referred to as a Search Engine and several dot-com companies, as they were later called, were frantically developing them.

Rob's company, called Greyhound, went public in 1994, one year before Alta Vista and two years before Yahoo. It was a feeding frenzy. In the first hour of trading the value of the company reached over $1 billion. By the end of the day Rob and his partners were the youngest multi-millionaires to so far emerge from Silicon Valley.

Rob was smart. He sensed the wave of new search engines being developed by other startup companies, so over the next two years he sold off his seventy-million dollars of stock on a regular monthly basis. By the time he was totally liquid, he had paid the government thirty million in taxes; however, he had forty million in the bank. He invested the money in bonds paying 8% and was realizing an income of over $3 million a year. He stayed with the company for another year but eventually left before the dot-com bubble burst in the late 1990's.

One of the few things that interested Rob besides computers was flying. Brett was his mentor. He had started talking to him about aviation back when Rob was starting his company. Brett had taken him up in his Baron several times and had put him in touch with Jim, Brett's previous flight instructor. Somehow Rob worked flying into his twenty hour a day schedule and earned a pilot license before his company went public.

In 1997, after Rob had left the company, he purchased only three things with his fortune: a house in the Los Altos hills, a BMW 328i, and a

Twin Engine Piper Seneca airplane. By 1999 he had built a thousand hours in the complex twin and traded it in on a Cessna Citation CJ1, one of the few jet airplanes certified to be flown with only a single pilot.

Six months ago Rob was seated in the dental chair filling Brett in on his new airplane. "Doc, you have to ride in this beast, it's unbelievable; it cruises between 350 and 400 knots."

Brett was impressed. "That's between four and five hundred miles an hour."

"Yeah, but remember that's up at about 30,000 ft. It's a little slower if we're going down to Monterey for a hamburger."

"Have you had a chance to take it on a long trip yet?"

"My instructor and I took it up to Anchorage. Two thousand miles, one stop, little over five hours."

"Wow," Brett said. "How many people fit in it?"

"It can seat seven including the pilot, but we have to leave some fuel out which means less range and more stops."

"That's pretty much the same for all airplanes. When do I get a ride?"

Rob was excited to show off his skills and his plane to his mentor. "Anytime, Doc, anytime. I have it hangared at San Jose Airport, just give me call. I'm always looking for an excuse to fly it."

Brett looked up Rob's cell phone number and placed the call. He answered on the first ring. "Rob."

"Hi, Rob. It's Brett Raven."

"Hey, Doc. What's up?"

"I'd like to take you up on that offer for a jet plane ride."

Rob was smiling. "I'm ready, when?"

"How 'bout tomorrow morning?"

"That'll work, meet me at the Jet Center around nine-thirty. We'll go down to Palm Springs for lunch."

"Sounds like fun. Mind if I bring a friend?"

"More the merrier."

"We'll be there at nine-thirty. By the way, I've got an adventure you might be interested in. I'll tell you about it over lunch."

"I could use an adventure, I'm bored stiff. See you tomorrow."

Brett spotted Rob in the lobby of the Jet Center. He took Annie's hand and led her inside. "Hi, Rob, this is Annie. She used to be my wife, now she's my girlfriend."

Annie shot Brett a dirty look. "Nice to see you again, Rob. I worked in the front office when you first came in for dental appointments."

Rob laughed. "I remember, you were the one who gave me the gold star after my check-up."

"That'd be me," Annie replied.

Brett interrupted, "Hey, let's go flying."

Rob led them out to the ramp and up to the sleek, white, personal jet. The entry door on the left side of the aircraft was open and supported three stairs which led to the cabin. "Go ahead up, Annie, and take one of the rear seats. Doc will be the co-pilot up front with me."

Annie sunk into one of the deep soft leather seats. Rob settled into the left pilot seat and Brett took his place in the right one.

Rob handed Brett the check list and the instrument flight plan. "Doc, run me through the check list, then the clearances and radios are yours."

Brett fulfilled his duties and received their instrument clearance from San Jose to Palm Springs. Rob taxied to the end of runway three zero and Brett announced to the tower, "Citation 68 Charlie Lima ready for IFR release."

The controller came back, "8 Charlie Lima, cleared for takeoff."

Rob, lined up with the center line, advanced the two throttles, and within ten minutes they were at 21,000 ft. headed for Palm Springs.

Flying distance between San Jose and Palm Springs was four hundred twenty-one miles and it only took them an hour and fifteen minutes before they taxied up to the general aviation terminal.

AMR-Combs, the operator of the terminal

provided a courtesy shuttle service and Rob instructed the driver to take them to the Cedar Creek Inn, about two miles away. After getting seated at an outside table in the courtyard, Rob asked, "How do you like the bird?"

Annie said, "Unbelievable."

Brett chimed in, "Fantastic."

Rob and Brett ordered hamburgers and Annie opted for a Cobb Salad. The guys had cokes since they were flying and Annie called for a Corona.

Brett started up the conversation again. "What are the hourly costs on the Citation?"

Rob thought for a minute. "For the speed we get the fuel costs are actually pretty reasonable. It uses 134 gallons an hour. Right now jet fuel is going for a little under two dollars, so it comes to about two hundred and fifty an hour."

"What do the costs go to when you add maintenance, taxes, and insurance?"

"It's probably around seven-fifty, but shit, what else do I have to spend my money on."

Everybody dug into the food that had been placed on the table. Finally Rob asked, "So what's the adventure you have for me?"

Brett washed the sandwich down with the soft drink and then pulled his chair closer to the table so other patrons wouldn't hear their conversation. "It's pretty complicated and you don't need to know all the dirty details, but I'll give you an overview so you'll know what you're in for if you decide to join us. An ex-friend of ours cheated us and several insurance companies out of a lot of money. We're going to get it back. I've worked out a plan, and it includes a jet plane and a pilot."

"I read the papers. This ex-friend wouldn't be your ex-partner would it?"

Annie spoke, "Ex-partner, ex-friend, ex-husband."

Rob's eyes lit up. He hadn't had any excitement in his life since the company had gone public six years ago. "So how do I fit in?"

"Your part will be twofold. One, you're our transportation. After a briefing meeting with the other players involved, we'll all pile into your plane and you'll fly us to West Palm Beach, Florida. Once we're there you'll take on the persona of a corporate pilot for a big money guy operating out of Palm Beach. You'll fly this guy and his friends anywhere they want to go. When we're ready to leave Florida, we'll want to make a hasty exit. You'll have the plane ready to get us all out of there."

Rob was literally drooling with excitement. "You're shitting me; this is too good to be true."

Brett was all business. "It's going to happen, Rob. Think you want a part of it?"

"Are you kidding me, absolutely!"

"Okay, let's talk finances. You said your costs in the Citation are about seven hundred-fifty an hour. I'll cover your hourly costs, your lodging, and meals for as long as we need to stay down there."

"Brett, I don't need that. You cover the fuel, two-fifty an hour and I'll pick up the other   costs. My insurance, maintenance and taxes are already paid.

Flying for you isn't going to increase those. If you want to cover the ramp and parking fees, that's fine."

"That's very generous Rob. If I'd known you were that eager, I'd have squeezed you a little more. This was too easy."

Everybody laughed and Annie leaned over and kissed Rob on the cheek, "It's going to be a blast," she said, as she drained the last drop from her Corona.

CHAPTER 19

It had been nineteen days since Brett's meeting with Drake Caymen. He was just finishing his second cup of coffee, and Annie was still in bed, when he heard his cell phone ringing in the den. He jumped off the stool at the breakfast counter and hustled to answer the phone. "Brett."

"Hey, Brett, Drake here. Did I get you out of bed?"

"No, no, I was just having breakfast. What have you got?"

"Some good stuff, I think you'll be pleased. Do you want it over the phone or by fax?"

Brett's stomach filled with butterflies anticipating Drake's findings. "Let's have it right now. You can send a fax later."

"Okay, first of all he is going by the name of Antonio Russ, not a giant step away from Tony Russo. I'm guessing it makes it easy to remember and can always be explained off as a typo if he makes a mistake."

"What about his wife?"

"No change, she's still Maria but obviously Maria Russ."

Brett grabbed a yellow pad and started jotting down notes. "Where they living?"

"Right where we thought, West Palm. They're renting a luxury condo in an upscale neighborhood. I'll give you the address in the fax."

"Any idea what they're paying?"

"Sure do. They have a one year lease at $3,800 a month that began on September 1, 2000, and terminates on August 31, 2001."

Brett was trying to control his excitement. "Did you have your associates monitor them at all?"

"Oh yeah, definitely. Antonio has coffee and reads his newspaper almost every morning at a Starbucks two blocks from his condo. He goes out to the West Palm airport two or three times a week, kicks the tires on some airplanes and bullshits with the local pilots. Once a week he drops in at the local Merrill Lynch office. The rest of the time he hangs around the pool."

"That's good work, Drake. What about Maria?"

"She was easy. Has an appointment every two weeks to have her nails done and another every two weeks for a pedicure. Has her hair done near the first of every month at a pricey salon. She must have standing appointments because they're on the same day and at the same time each week."

Brett was furiously taking notes. "Do they have any social life?"

"Not much. In the two and half weeks we watched them, they never met with any other couples and neither of them seem to have individual friends."

"Do they eat out at all?"

"Yeah, about three or four times a week. They have a couple favorite spots and look like regulars there. They always eat alone, never with other couples or singles."

"Anything else?"

There was silence; Drake was obviously pondering the question. "They seemed to be pretty relaxed. It didn't appear they were worried that someone might be watching them. You know, no looking over their shoulder, no evasive maneuvers."

"Drake, this is even better than I had hoped for. Go ahead and fax me the info at 650-555-3434 at exactly ten a.m. Pacific Time. I'll be at the machine to collect it."

"Will do," Drake said.

"It took longer than we thought; I must owe you some more cash."

"Yeah, looks like another twenty-two hundred bucks."

Brett wrote down $2,200. "I'll drop a money

order in the mail. By the way, I think I may have more work for you. Any problem with a little travel?"

"I love to travel, just let me know what you need."

"I'll call you in the next couple weeks," Brett said, and clicked off the cellphone.

He got up from his desk and saw Annie in the doorway. She could tell Brett had been talking to Drake. "Good news?"

Brett grinned and replied, "We're in business."

CHAPTER 20

Brett was at the dental office going through his usual motions when the intercom in his office buzzed. "Hi, Ginger. What's up?"

"A fat man with a crew cut and a card naming him Biff has blessed us with his presence. Do you want me to send him on his way?"

"No, escort him back to my office."

Ginger turned to Biff and very officiously said, "You're lucky. Normally people need appointments to see the doctor, but apparently he likes you and will see you. Follow me."

Ginger knocked on the door and opened it before any response was forthcoming. Brett stood up from his chair and greeted the investigator.

"Hello, Elmer. What brings you into the territory of the enemy?"

Biff displayed none of the bravado or arrogance that he had at their first meeting.

"Brett, may I sit down with you for a few minutes?"

Brett motioned him to the recliner he had pulled up near his desk. Biff settled into it and Brett took his usual seat at his desk. "May I call you Biff?'

"If it makes you more comfortable to piss me off with Elmer, go ahead, but let's cut the bullshit and talk."

Brett became serious. "Okay Biff, I'm guessing you have important business or you wouldn't be here."

Biff clasped his hands together and rested them on his enormous belly. "Brett, I have most of the fraud figured out. I'd like to run my theory by you."

Brett was curious to find out how much Biff had put together. "I'm all ears."

"Okay, you had a best friend named J.T. Talbot, who was also your partner in a twin engine airplane. Something happened between you and your wife and she divorced you five years ago in 1995. J.T., being the good friend that he was, married your ex-wife. That didn't exactly strengthen your friendship with him. In fact you rarely talked to him during the next five years. How am I doing so far?"

"Keep going," Brett replied.

"J.T. lost a ton of money on a stock deal. He also took on the identity of an old client named Tony Russo, and married a gal in Minnesota while he was still married to your ex, Annie." Biff paused.

"Keep going," Brett said again.

"Well it seems J.T. went on a fishing trip with another guy down to Baja, and on the way back he crashed your airplane and both of them were killed."

"So far it sounds like you have it right. What else?"

Biff was feeling a little smug now and he continued. "Well, here's the strange part. The two guys who officially died in the crash were J.T. Talbot and Tony Russo. How could that be if they were actually the same guy?"

"I give up, how?"

"Well, there were two dead guys in that plane all right, but neither one was J.T. nor Tony. Your best buddy escaped, but the insurance companies didn't know that. They paid Annie a huge life insurance claim and you an airplane claim. Maria, Tony's wife, ended up with five and a half million. That's the money we're both looking for."

Brett was impressed. Biff was definitely smarter than he looked. "So where does that leave us?"

"The insurance companies didn't question the accident, but you figured it out. Then you tracked J.T. down, but the bastard and his wife gave you the slip. Any idea where they are?"

"Where do you think they are?"

"That's my problem. You're the only one who has any idea, and I think you're getting close."

"Biff, I don't get it. Are you here just to tell me

what I already know?"

"Not exactly, I wanted you to know what I know. If you recover the money, you get the ten percent. I'm good with that, but I've been offered a hundred thousand bonus if I can bring J.T. back to face charges. How 'bout you turn him over to me after you get the dough."

Brett was thinking. He had nothing to lose if Biff took J.T. into custody after the money was recovered. The problem he had was believing Biff would be satisfied with such a small piece of the pie. He didn't trust him and wasn't about to give him any information at this point. "I'll have to think about it," he said.

Biff got out of his chair. "What do you have to lose?"

"To be honest, I don't know if I can trust you. I'm afraid you'll fuck up the whole deal and leave me holding the bag."

"How can I gain your trust?"

Brett wanted to say, "Start by staying out of my garbage" but instead replied, "Like I said, I'll have to think about it. I have your card, I'll be in touch."

Biff offered his hand and Brett shook it. "I'll wait for your call," Biff said, and then he was gone.

CHAPTER 21

Brett gave Enrique a call, "Everybody still in?" He asked.

"Yeah, been wondering when you'd call. What's up?"

"I want a meeting at our house to finalize the deal and set the time schedule. When's good for you guys?"

"Just name a time," Enrique replied.

"How about tomorrow night around seven-thirty? We're in San Carlos, up Club Drive to 44 Geranium Lane."

"I know the area, anything we should bring?"

"Just you, Manny, the ladies, and do you think you could bring Omar along?"

"You mean tomorrow or on the trip?"
"Both." Brett replied.
"He'll love it. See you tomorrow night."

At seven-thirty sharp, two jet black Cadillacs
with grey smoked windows pulled into the parking
lot next to the townhouse. Enrique and a beautiful
woman about fifty years old with light brown skin,
black hair and brown eyes got out of one car while
Manny and a younger lady about thirty-five, also
dark, and equally beautiful, emerged from the
second vehicle. Omar jumped out of the back seat
of Manny's car and all five came to the front door
together.

Both Annie and Brett were at the door to greet
them. "Hello everyone, thanks so much for coming.
Let's go into the living room and get acquainted."

Just as everyone started for the other room,
Rob knocked on the door and Annie greeted him
with a hug.

Everyone settled into seats. "Let's get to know
each other; we're going to spend a lot of time
together in the next couple months. You all know
I'm Brett and this is Annie."

The older woman smiled and said, "And I'm
Marcella, Enrique's wife."

The younger woman added, "And I'm Carmen,
Manny's girlfriend."

Annie and Brett got up and made the rounds.

"It's so nice to meet you Marcella….Carmen, and Omar it's nice to have you onboard.

Brett pointed to Rob, "This is Rob. He, like me, is a pilot; only he has the distinction of owning and flying a Cessna Citation private jet."

Rob gave a little nod. Enrique reached over, shook Rob's hand and said, "I'm Enrique, this is Manny and Omar." The other two men gave thumbs up. The ladies smiled.

"How 'bout drinks?" Annie asked.

"Scotch?' Enrique inquired.

"Chevas okay?'

"Great," Enrique replied

"Make it two," Manny chimed in.

"Make it three," Omar said in his deep baritone.

"Ladies?" Brett asked.

"Diet anything," Marcella replied.

"The same," Carmen added.

"Any beer is fine," Rob said.

Brett went to the bar and Annie to the kitchen. As Brett set down the drinks, Annie put out a nice Brie and some wheat crackers on the center of the coffee table.

Brett took a slug of his scotch and continued on with the conversation. "I assume that Enrique and Manny have outlined the operation to the ladies and Omar."

"As much as we know, which isn't much," Manny said.

Brett laughed, "I purposely haven't detailed every part of the plan to anyone except Annie. Let me start filling everyone in on some of the pieces. First of all we're planning on leaving for Palm Beach Florida in a month on the second of January. Will that work for everybody?"

Eyes moved from right to left and they all nodded the affirmative. I'm guessing we'll be down there for six to eight weeks. Everyone still okay with it?"

Again all the heads went up and down.

"Okay, let's begin. If everything goes to plan, we're going to have a lot of fun, a great vacation, and since you're doing all the work, you'll make a lot of money. Annie and I are only going to get repaid for monies that we lost and for our expenses."

"I like the money part," Enrique said.

"Is that all you think about? I'm looking forward to the beach and the sun," Marcella replied.

Brett laughed; he was beginning to like Marcella. "Our transportation will be first class; Rob's plane holds seven. Going east everyone except Annie will be aboard. Coming back someone will have to ride commercial."

A deep voice boomed out, "That'll be me," Omar volunteered.

"Perfect," Brett said, and then continued. "We'll have to make stops for fuel going down, but the trip still won't take long; the Citation cruises at nearly five hundred miles an hour."

Carmen, who hadn't said a word asked, "Why isn't Annie coming?"

"She'll join us there; she has another assignment

to complete before she meets up with us in Palm Beach," Brett replied. "Rob will drop us off in Miami and we'll pick up some luxury cars. The ladies will love the next part. We're going on a shopping spree. I want Enrique, Manny, Marcella and Carmen to look like they belong in wealthy Palm Beach; lots of silk, linen and cotton and, of course, ladies, shoes."

"Yea," Carmen hooted,

"Rob, you can do your shopping here. All you need is a pilot outfit complete with epaulets and a captain's hat. Once we're there, the jet will belong to Enrique and you'll just be a corporate pilot on call."

"You mean I don't get any linens or new shoes?" Rob asked jokingly.

"I know you, Rob; the last thing you need is linens. Omar, unfortunately all you get is some new khakis and a blue blazer with a bulge in its pocket."

"Those are dress up clothes for me," Omar replied.

Brett laughed and continued, "We'll drive from Miami to Palm Beach; it's only seventy miles. Rob will bring the jet to West Palm Beach where the airport is located."

"Where we staying once we get there?" Manny asked.

"Here's the best part. I've leased a two acre estate on the ocean. The main house is full of bedrooms. Enrique and Marcella will take one master and Manny and Carmen will take the other.

There's a guest house which Annie and I will take, and there's a great pool house that Rob will love. Omar is the last man in, so the poor guy is stuck with the beach house."

"Is this for real?" Carmen asked.

Brett smiled again, "It's for real but it's not all fun and games. They'll be work to do."

Annie interrupted, "Let's take a break. Everyone's drinks are empty and no one has touched the food."

Brett smiled at Annie; she was right to pause the conversation. It was going to take time for everyone to process this operation in their minds.

The men mingled next to the bar and the women went into the kitchen to get some more food. By the time all the glasses were freshened up and some hot hors d'oeuvres were placed on the table, Brett was ready to continue and his guests were eager to listen. "Where was I? Oh yeah, the work. Everyone has a part to play in this operation. Enrique is going to be a big time Colombian drug dealer and his new name is going to be Carlos Alberto Rojas. To keep it easy, Marcella, his wife will keep her same name. Manny will be a Cuban professional loan broker who handles all the financing for Carlos. He'll keep the name Emanuel or Manny, but his last name is now Diaz. Carmen will be his wife and she'll keep her own first name."

Carmen chimed in, "Did you hear the wife part Manny?"

Everybody laughed except Manny.

"Rob, you are Carlos' personal pilot and you'll

fly him in his private jet wherever he needs to go. In actuality I'll be the one giving out the destinations. Omar will just be Omar; he's Carlos' bodyguard."

Enrique had been listening and not talking much. Finally he asked, "What's the point of the charade?"

"Okay, the point of all this luxury and opulence is to impress two people, Antonio and Maria Russ. I want them to soak it all in and to want this same kind of lifestyle for themselves. They're very impressed by wealth and it won't take much to bait the hook. Marcella and Carmen will be our marketing team. We'll make sure they meet Maria and they'll strike up a friendship and invite her and Antonio to the estate. Antonio's mouth will water to be friends with Carlos and Manny. That's our goal.

Enrique asked the next obvious question, "How are we going to do all that?"

"I'm going to tell you how, piece by piece as we go along. Every morning at breakfast, we'll have a meeting. If action is going to take place that day, we'll rehearse everyone's parts. I'm purposely not giving you the entire script because I want each of you to only be concerned with what will happen that day. If nothing is happening on a given day," Brett looked at Marcella, "You can hit that beach you're looking forward to."

Marcella gave a weak smile, "Brett, we're not actresses, how are we going to do this?"

"You and Carmen just have to imagine that you're filthy rich and then be who you already are. We want Maria to like you, and being yourself will put her at ease. A lot of this is going to be just show: two acre estate, jet plane, luxury cars, clothes, jewelry. By the way you'll both need lots of jewelry. If you need more, we'll buy some imitation stuff."

"I have plenty," Marcella said, "Enrique is very generous."

Carmen looked at Manny again, "I don't have much." Manny rolled his eyes.

Marcella said, "Don't worry; I have enough for both of us."

"Great," Brett said. "Don't worry about the acting part; I'm convinced you both can pull it off."

"One important thing to remember at all times," Brett added, "is that Antonio can never get a glimpse of Annie or me. If he does, the entire operation is blown. Whenever he comes to the estate, Annie and I will be gone and Manny and Carmen won't appear to be living there. Rob and Omar can stay in their respective cottages; that looks natural enough."

"Doc, I think you're wasting your time drilling teeth," Manny said. "I better be careful or Enrique will be offering you my job."

"I'll take that as some sort of compliment," Brett replied. "One last thing; when we're finished, we leave quickly. Omar will take one car to Miami and get an airline ticket home, and we'll return the other two at the West Palm airport. Rob will already have the Citation ready to go. We jump in and 'poof' we're gone."

"Hey, nobody has touched the food," Annie

exclaimed.

"Maybe it's the butterflies in our stomachs," Marcella said.

Brett was concerned, "Hey, everybody, what's the worst that can happen? Antonio and Maria don't go for it, we're unsuccessful, and we all come home on a private jet with a tan. Annie and I are paying all the expenses; we're the only ones that can lose anything."

There was silence for a moment and then everyone broke into laughter. Brett joined in and said, "We'll have all the props for you; cell phones, business cards, an office for Manny, appointments for the ladies. All you have to do is show up, do your best, and have some fun. Any questions?"

No one spoke up. "Okay everybody, let's have another drink and eat some of this food Annie prepared. Our next get-together will be at the San Jose Jet Center on January 2nd at six a.m."

CHAPTER 22

It was Thursday and that meant the night Brett would be putting out the garbage cans. He sat down at his computer and wrote a letter to himself.

Brett,

I heard you're looking for me so you can pick up a million dollars in reward money. I don't want you nosing around, so I'm willing to pay you the million dollars you're after just to get you off my back. If you're interested, put an ad in the personals of the San Francisco Chronicle on December 10th. Address it to Long Lost Friend and say "eager to see you again." I'll respond the next day, same place.

J.T.

He took the letter out of his printer and rolled it up in a ball. Then he opened it up and tore it in half lengthwise and again crosswise. He went down to the garage and opened the blue recycle garbage can which contained newspapers, cans, plastic, and torn up junk mail. He took out some of the junk mail, tore them in half, and mixed the four pieces of his letter with the scraps. Then he carefully placed his little pile on top of the other items and spread it out randomly.

After putting the cans out in front of the garage, Brett went back to his office and marked his calendar to remind him to call the Chronicle before the 5th to ensure his ad would appear on the 10th. Then he set the clock radio next to his bed for four a.m.

Brett had forgotten to turn the volume down and Annie jumped up in bed, "What the..."

"Annie, Annie, it's okay; I'm just going to check on our buddy." She flopped her head back down on the pillow and was breathing deeply as Brett got up to position himself near the front window.

Biff didn't disappoint. At four-twenty he walked up the cul-de-sac while staying in the shadows of the other units. He looked in both directions and then opened the recycle can. He scooped up all the torn papers and mail which Brett had spread out and then he rummaged below and put a few more scraps he found there into his sack. He looked around again and satisfied that he hadn't been seen, slipped back into the shadows and quickly re-traced his way back to the main street. Brett smiled to himself and dropped back into bed.

CHAPTER 23

This was their second visit to LGTI. After their first visit, Annie had phoned Liz and told her they were ready to move forward. Today's appointment was to meet a surrogate who had been chosen for them to interview.

Liz emerged from her office and greeted them in the waiting room. "Hello, Annie, hello, Brett, I'm so glad you've decided to go ahead. I think you're going to really like Samantha. Come into my office I'll introduce you."

Liz led the way, followed by Annie, with Brett bringing up the rear. As they entered the office, a very plain looking young lady rose to her feet. She looked to be about thirty years old, slightly overweight, and dressed in a brown pair of slacks and a tan blouse. Brett thought to himself; if she were in a room with twenty people, she'd be the last person anyone would notice.

Liz extended her arm and raised her palm up. "Samantha, this is Annie and Brett, the couple I told you about."

Brett shook Samantha's hand and to everyone's surprise, Annie embraced her. Samantha hugged her back and said, "I truly hope I can be part of this with you."

"I'm going to leave you three alone to get acquainted," Liz said, as she slipped out the door.

Everyone took seats on the couches around the coffee table. There was an awkward silence which was finally broken by Samantha. "I'd like to tell you a little about myself. I'm thirty-one years old, married with three children."

"How old are the kids? "Annie asked.

"Nine, six, and three; I had the first when I was twenty-two." she responded.

"Ever been a surrogate before?" Brett asked.

"Actually I have. The delivery was thirteen months ago."

"I don't get it, Annie said." "You've been pregnant four times in nine years. Doesn't it get old?"

Samantha looked a little embarrassed with a hint of shame. "I like it."

"Oh, Samantha, I didn't mean it that way. We're so thankful for having you."

"It's okay," she said. "A lot of my friends think

I'm nuts, but it gives me pleasure."

"Does the money help?" Brett asked.

"I'd actually do it for free, but my husband wants to go back to graduate school and your money will make that possible."

Annie spoke, "Samantha, I want to apologize again. I didn't mean to insult..."

"Annie, I'm not insulted. I know I'm a little different than the average woman, but I'm okay with it."

Annie got up and went over to give her a hug. She looked over Samantha's shoulder at Brett. He gave her thumbs up.

"Samantha," Annie said, "We want you to carry our baby."

Samantha hugged her back tightly and let a torrent of the tears stream down her cheeks.

"Thank you," she said. "Thank you."

After their meeting with Samantha, Liz asked Annie and Brett to come into her private office. "We'll need some medical data. Annie, we need you to take some tests to determine if you are producing eggs. Brett, we need a semen sample from you to determine if you have active sperm. Our doctor has written the orders; you can complete these tests at a hospital near your home and have the results forwarded to us here."

Brett took the hospital orders and asked, "Is the process in motion?"

"If your tests are positive, we'll proceed. Annie will meet with our doctors and procedures for egg harvest will be scheduled. You'll need to provide a fresh semen sample to be used for the in vitro fertilization process."

"We haven't talked very much about the payment schedule," Brett said.

Liz replied, "We'll ask you for a $25,000 payment to move forward before the eggs are harvested. When the embryos are planted, we'll request a second $25,000 payment, and when the pregnancy is over, successful or not, we'll ask you for the balance."

"What's the time frame?" Annie asked.

Liz thought for a moment. "It will take a few weeks to get tests and results and then we're coming up on the holidays. I'd guess the middle of January for harvest and fertilization, and hopefully a pregnancy by early February."

Annie was silent but smiling as Brett maneuvered through the freeway traffic on the 101 as they headed home.

He looked over toward her. "You going to let me in?"

She gave a start. "Sorry. I'm just so happy. All of a sudden those feelings of shame and guilt from the past that have haunted me don't seem so important anymore. The thought of this baby is overtaking them."

"I'm really relieved to hear that. Do you think you can let go of it completely?"

Annie was pensive for a minute or two and then said, "I think I can. I really think I can."

CHAPTER 24

Annie was scrambling eggs as Brett trotted down the stairs toward the kitchen. "Are they ready yet?" He asked.

"Just about," Annie responded. "Chop that tomato for me, will you?"

Brett sliced the red fruit and then cut it into squares. He spied some fresh basil on the bottom shelf of the fridge, tore it into small pieces, and tossed it in with the tomato. Annie dished out the eggs and Brett topped them with his concoction while she set the plates on the breakfast counter with a basket of toast and a pot of coffee.

"Nice touch with the basil," Annie said, as she stuffed a forkful in her mouth.

"Thanks, saw it on T.V."

Annie laughed, "I don't see you watching the food channel."

"Morning news had that cooking guy with the big moustache on for about a thirty second spot. I watched it while I was shaving."

The eggs were gone in less than five minutes. "What are you doing for lunch?" Annie asked.

"I'm barely done with breakfast. What's the fixation on meals?" Brett responded.

"I ran into your old friend Trevor, the guy with the Baron. He asked why you stopped coming to the airport for lunch. I told him we were back together and he invited us to join him for lunch at the Sky Kitchen Café."

"Today?"

"Why not?"

"Sounds great; I'll meet you there at noon. What are you doing this morning?

"Duh, I have to go in for that GYN exam and then get a blood test."

"Oh, I forgot, sorry."

"I know they're going to send a bottle home for you."

"Yeah, I know. That will be a little embarrassing."

"If you're a good boy, I may help."

Brett smiled. "Now I'm looking forward to it."

Annie changed the subject. "You headed to the office?"

"Duh, I get my cast off at ten o'clock. Then

I'll head over and bring Ginger up to date on our vacation to Florida."

Annie kissed him. "Sorry, I forgot too. Good luck and remember, noon at the Sky Kitchen."

When Brett arrived at the office at ten forty-five; it had already been buzzing for almost three hours. Ginger spotted him in the parking lot and greeted him as he came in the side door. "You're late."

Brett laughed, "Like anybody notices, but you."

"Just don't want you to get into bad habits. It won't be long before you're back working, so get your chin up. Hey, you got your cast off. How's it feel?"

"A little stiff, but really pretty good. Nice to get rid of all that plaster. You have time for a chat?"

"Give me five minutes. Janet will have a break and can take over the desk for a while."

Ginger knocked on the door of the private office and walked in before Brett could respond. She took her usual seat in his recliner. "I'm always worried when we have these meetings. It usually means something big is about to happen."

"As a matter of fact something is." Brett responded.

"Don't tell me. The time has come to go back into battle against that jerk J.T."

"I wouldn't say battle. I'm hoping it'll be more like a cake walk."

"Brett, why can't you let go? What's in it for you?"

"Revenge, I guess."

"Why do you need revenge? The guy's a prick and you know it. Isn't that enough?"

"Ginger, I've got him by the balls and he doesn't have any idea what's about to hit him."

"What is about to hit him?"

Brett didn't answer the question and instead said, "Annie and I will be gone for a couple months."

"You're kidding, right?"

"I'll be in touch and we'll be back for a day or two every couple weeks."

"I don't suppose you're going to tell me where you're going."

"I can't. If you were to let it slip out, it would ruin everything."

"Okay then, how can I help?"

"Just keep the place going the way you always do and trust me. I know what I'm doing."

"Brett, you know I always trust you. I just worry about you."

"I know you do. Hey I'm going to let you in on a secret which should cheer you up."

"What?"

"Annie and I are going to have a baby. We're going through a surrogate."

Ginger jumped out of her chair and planted a kiss on Brett's cheek. "Oh Brett, that's so great. Can I say anything to Annie?"

"Let's just keep it low key for now."

"No problem, I understand. When are you leaving on this trip?"

"Six weeks, the second of January."

The intercom buzzed and Brett answered. "What's up Janet?"

"I need Ginger."

"She's on her way."

Ginger started for the door, and then turned back to Brett. "Be careful."

"Always," he said.

Before J.T. crashed his airplane in Baja, Brett ate lunch in the Sky Kitchen Café almost every day. Since the loss of his plane he purposely avoided the diner; it was just too painful to meet with all the pilots and have to lie about the events that surrounded J.T. and the so called accident. As soon as he walked through the door, he realized how much he missed the pilot camaraderie that was going on at the center table of the café.

He spotted Trevor at the center counter along with two seats being saved for him and Annie. Brett slapped him on the back, "Hey, Trevor."

"Brett, God damn, it's been a long time. How the hell are you?"

"Pretty good. Just got the cast off my hand this morning."

"Yeah, tough luck. First J.T. crashes the plane and then you get mugged. Guess you had a bad month."

"I'm doing fine."

Just then Trevor spotted Annie coming in and motioned her to the last saved seat. "Hi guys," Annie said.

Trevor jumped up and gave her a peck on the cheek. "Jeez, it's great having you two back together. I've missed you guys."

"Thanks, Trev, it's been great for us."

Brett leaned over to Annie and whispered, "How did the doctor appointment go?"

"They think I'm putting out eggs by the dozen. I brought you your bottle."

A half dozen other pilots came up to Brett and Annie, exchanging greetings and in some cases condolences for J.T. After ordering some lunch, Trevor spoke. "That Baron J.T. crashed was the big 58 model, wasn't it?"

"Yeah, it was a beauty," Brett said nostalgically.

"Didn't you fly the smaller 55 for a while?"

"That was J.T.'s first Baron. It was a B model with the two small 260 horse power engines. I earned my multi engine rating in it."

Trevor pushed his plate aside. "I put a deposit down on a 58. You interested in buying my 55?"

Brett's eyes lit up. "Which model is it?"

"It's actually a D model. Looks exactly like the B model, can seat six and all, but it has the big 285 horse power engines. It screams at 200 knots; at least 230 mph."

"I'm interested," Brett said.

Annie, who had remained silent said, "We're interested."

"Let's go over to the hangar, you can look it over." Trevor said.

As soon as the door slid open it was love at first sight. The plane was pristine. Even though it was thirty years old, it looked as if it had just rolled off the assembly line. It was glossy white with three stripes of purple, blue and gold running along the sides of the fuselage from nose to tail. The Plexiglas windows were all new and glistened as the sun bounced off them.

Brett climbed up on the wing and looked inside. The six seats were done in beige leather and the carpets were off white. The instrument panel was state of the art and included a Garmin GPS unit and a King auto-pilot with a flight director, along with all the other standard radio equipment. In the center was a Strike Finder used to detect weather up ahead. Brett noticed that all the headsets were noise cancelling and a stereo music system had been installed and tied into them.

"Want to take it for a spin?" Trevor asked.

"That would be great."

Trevor attached the motor tow and wheeled the bird out of the hangar. He spent about ten minutes doing a pre-flight inspection and then handed the keys to Brett. "Have fun," he said.

"Whoa, Trev, I can't take your plane out without you in it."

"Why not? How many Baron hours do you have?"

"Over a thousand, but…"

"Are you current?"

"Yeah, I flew one to Baja a couple months ago. Put about fifteen hours on it."

"Have fun," he said again, and walked off in the direction of the Sky Kitchen.

Brett looked at Annie. Annie looked at Brett, and they both broke out laughing. "Let's go," Annie said.

Brett got in first and took the left seat; Annie slid into the right while snapping the door handle into the locked position. After attaching their belts, Brett took out the familiar check list and worked through it. Finally he hit the boost pump for the left engine and fired it up. When he had oil pressure in the left engine, he hit the boost for the right engine and followed the same procedure for the start. The sound of the two propellers winding in opposite directions was like a symphony to his ears, and he gave Annie a wide smile and a thumbs up.

Brett hit the avionics switch, bringing all the instruments, radios, and intercom to life. "Ever seen the Farallon Islands up close?" He asked.

"You kidding? They're thirty miles west of the Golden Gate Bridge. There's a lot of water out there."

"We've got two engines. You okay with it?"

"Is it legal to fly out there?"

"I'll get permission. You up for it?"

"Let's go."

After getting takeoff clearance, Brett advanced

the two throttles and barreled down the twenty-six hundred foot runway. He rotated the nose when his speed reached eighty-five knots and the Baron lifted off the blacktop. Then he trimmed the climb angle for a hundred and ten knots and established a climb rate of twelve hundred feet per minute.

Brett didn't need any navigation equipment to locate the Woodside Vortac Beacon; it was the common reporting check point to the west, and he had flown over it at least a thousand times. Being careful not to penetrate restricted airspace, Brett leveled off at fifteen hundred feet and headed for Woodside. He dialed 135.1. "NorCal Approach, Baron six, seven, five, nine, Mike, at fifteen hundred over Woodside VOR."

"Baron five, nine, Mike, this is NorCal. Go ahead."

"Five, nine, Mike requests permission to fly the Woodside two seven zero radial direct to the Farallon islands."

"Squawk 3550 on your transponder and maintain VFR outside the class B airspace."

Brett dialed the number into his unit. "Squawking 3550," he responded.

About two minutes passed before the controller came back to him. "Baron five, nine, Mike, radar contact four miles west of the Woodside VOR. Keep in mind there's an Air Defense Identification Zone just to the west of the islands. Do not penetrate that boundary."

"I've set it into the GPS. I'll stay clear."

"Keep the same code and call us when you start

back toward shore," responded the controller. "Good flight."

"Affirm," Brett said, as he climbed up to forty-five hundred feet and reduced his engines to low cruise power.

Annie was overwhelmed by the expanse of the blue Pacific Ocean which looked endless as they headed due west. "It's breathtaking; looks as if it stretches into infinity," she said.

"It really is, isn't it? Hey, there're the islands straight ahead."

"Looks like a bunch of rocks."

"I think in Spanish, Farallons actually mean rocks out of the sea."

Annie laughed, "I guess I was absent the day they taught that."

Brett slowed the plane and dropped down to two thousand feet. "This is as low as we can go. It's a nature preserve down there."

"Pretty barren, and oh my God, I've never seen so many birds and bird shit in one place," Annie said.

"Yeah, you'd stick to the rocks if you walked on them; they're much prettier from a distance."

Brett circled the three main rocky islands twice. "I'm going to circle back to West End Island. Supposedly there's a shipwreck from the forties down there."

Brett swung the Baron to a two eight five heading and when he reached West End turned to three five zero and paralleled the island. "There, down there," he said. "You can see metal sticking out of the water."

Annie squinted. "I'll be damned; there it is. What are those buildings down there? I thought the islands were uninhabited."

"I think they're part of a marine research station. I guess some crazy scientists actually spend time out here. Hey, I've got a great idea. When was the last time you flew over the Golden Gate Bridge and Alcatraz?"

"Probably just after you got your license; when we were married and not living in sin."

"I said I wouldn't pressure you, remember?"

"I appreciate it. Are you headed for the bridge?"

"Yeah, I'll give NorCal a call."

Brett still had 135.1 illuminated in his number one radio. "NorCal Approach, Baron six, seven, five, nine, Mike. Farallons at two thousand."

"Five, nine, Mike, NorCal Approach. You headed back?"

"Affirmative, but we're going to come in through the bay."

"Roger that. Contact NorCal Approach on 120.9

"Twenty point nine. Five, nine, Mike."

Brett set the new frequency into his number two radio. "NorCal, Baron six, seven, five, nine, Mike, with you at two thousand."

"Five, nine, Mike, remain VFR, clear of class B airspace."

Brett acknowledged and turned the Baron to a zero, seven, zero heading and climbed to thirty-five hundred feet. In less than ten minutes the Bridge was in his windshield. "I'm going to drop back down to fifteen hundred," he said to Annie.

"Roger that," Annie responded with a giggle.

Brett slowed the plane down to a hundred knots and cruised over the Golden Gate. "How lucky we are," Annie said.

Brett smiled. It felt great to be back again at the controls of an airplane. Alcatraz came up in less than a minute as Brett turned the Baron to head down the Bay on the west side of the Oakland Airport. Just then the radio came alive. "Baron, five, nine, Mike, contact the Oakland North Tower on 118.3."

"One eighteen three. Five, nine, Mike"

Brett set the digits into his number one radio. "Oakland North Tower, Baron five, nine, Mike is with you at fifteen hundred for San Carlos."

"Good afternoon five, nine, Mike. Fly to the mid span of the San Mateo Bridge at or below fourteen hundred, stay clear of Class B."

"At or below fourteen. Five, nine, Mike"

Brett complied with instructions and after being switched to the Oakland south tower, he was turned over to San Carlos. He was cleared to land, squeaked the wheels onto the runway and taxied back to the hangar where Trevor was waiting. "How did it go?" he asked, as Annie jumped off the wing.

"Great," Annie answered.

"Pretty sweet, Trev," Brett added.

"When do you want to take possession?"

"Whoa, we haven't even talked price."

"Annie negotiated the deal. She's buying it for you."

Brett's mouth fell open. "Where did you get the money?"

"I gave Trevor my last twenty thousand to hold it for three months. His new plane won't be here till then anyway."

Trevor joined in. "Annie told me you're expecting a big payday in a couple months. If it doesn't happen, I'll give Annie her deposit back."

Brett gave Annie a hug. "Now I really want Florida to work out for us."

"It will," Annie said. "It will."

CHAPTER 25

Brett sequestered himself in his private office with instructions not be disturbed. Today was housekeeping day for him. He had to make sure the nuts and bolts were in place for their trip in four weeks.

Brett had over seven hundred thousand dollars in his private retirement plan, which had to be tapped in order to raise the money for the operation. His lawyer had already drawn up the papers and Brett had signed them. The plan loaned him two hundred fifty thousand dollars for a hundred and twenty months at six percent simple interest. If the operation in Florida failed, Brett would have to come up with $2,775 every month for the next ten years to pay back the loan.

He opened up his personal check book where he

had deposited the money. The first check he had written was to J. Granville & Associates for seventy-five hundred. That secured office space for three months. The second one, the big one, was to Hathaway Properties for ninety-eight thousand five hundred. Ten thousand of it was a refundable deposit; however, it still had taken a major chunk from his budget. The caveat: the estate was theirs for three months. The only other check written out of the account was for eighty-two hundred dollars to Vince Moreno for his legal services.

Brett had scanned the internet and found a small private bank in Florida, Miami Bank & Trust. He gave them a call and requested the senior vice president. "Peter Rankin, what can I do for you?" a voice boomed.

"My name is Brett Raven, Mr. Rankin. We're out in California and we're setting up a loan brokerage firm in West Palm Beach next month. "Any chance you could use a five million dollar deposit?"

Peter laughed. "My wife will love the bonus. What's the deal? Hope there's no drug money."

"No, these are legitimate, traceable funds. They were received as benefits from insurance companies about three months ago."

"I have to be real careful here in Florida, Mr. Raven, when I accept a large deposit like that."

"I understand. If you can jot down this name and number; Ralph Phillips, 415-555-7500. He's the Western United States Manager for Connecticut Mutual Life and he'll send you any documentation you need to put your mind at ease that the money is legitimate."

"That's great. I'll give him a call and then I'll get back to you with the routing number for the wire transfer."

"Perfect," Brett said. "By the way, we'll need a set of three on a page business checks. I'll fax the info down."

"Well, you've made my day, Mr. Raven."

"Call me Brett," he said.

"Okay. Thanks Brett."

After hanging up from the Miami Bank & Trust, he made a call to Vince Moreno. "Brett, I haven't heard much from you. Is the deal still on?"

"Sure is, and by the way, I'm calling in that favor Ralph Phillips promised."

"What is it?"

"He'll get a call today from a Miami banker, Peter Rankin. He just has to vouch for the source of the five million dollars."

"That should be no problem, since the money is clean. Anything else I can do?"

"Yeah, get me Ralph's private number and tell him to expect a call from me in January. I'm going to need his help one more time."

"I'll do that. Try to keep me in the loop, but on the outside edge."

"Will do. Thanks a lot Vince."

Brett threw his notes in a briefcase and strolled toward the front desk. Ginger looked up and said, "Pretty secretive back there."

"Believe me, you don't want to know. Hey,

I'm headed down to the stationery store, need anything?"

"We're good. See you later."

Brett looked through the business card section. He decided on a plain white card with a raised embossed surface for his first selection. He wrote out the inscription on an order slip.

Carlos Alberto Rojas
South Caribbean Imports
2555 South Ocean Blvd
Palm Beach, Fl. 33480
561-555-9989

His second pick was a beige card with a linen finish.

Emanuel Diaz
Creative Lending & Management
2727 Okeechobee Blvd.
West Palm Beach, Fl. 33401
772-555-3846

When he placed the order, he included stationery and envelopes for each business. On the way back to the office he gave Annie a call. "How you doing?"

"No morning sickness, if that's what you mean."

"Guess that's one advantage of a surrogate. Hey, let's go out to dinner and celebrate."

"Celebrate what?"

"Tomorrow we wire five million one hundred

and ninety thousand dollars to Florida."

"We going to have enough left for dinner?"

"I think so. I'll make a reservation at Kincaids."

"Okay, be home by five."

CHAPTER 26

Kincaid's Bayhouse is located adjacent to the San Francisco Bay in Burlingame. It only took fifteen minutes to drive there from their townhouse and Brett parked his new Lexus next to one of the old railroad ties which were set along the parking lot's periphery. They headed straight to the bar.

Kincaid's bar was the most impressive either one of them had ever seen. The bottles stretched from floor to the ceiling and a sliding ladder was needed just for the bartenders to navigate up through the inventory. Brett had to help Annie onto a bar stool. She was only five feet tall and the stool seats were at least three and a half feet off the floor. "What sounds good?" he asked.

"Maybe a Margarita up."

Brett ordered a Prima Mango Margarita for Annie and a Makers Mark neat for himself.

"Going with the hard stuff tonight?" Annie asked.

"Tough day at the office."

"You wish. You're dying for a tough day at the office."

"A couple more months," he said.

The drinks were set in front of them. Brett handed the Margarita to Annie and took the old fashion glass with light brown liquid for himself. Holding his glass in the air, he said, "To success in Florida, at least one new baby in a crib, and a new airplane in the hangar."

Annie tapped her glass to his. "To all of that."

"Did you hear from Liz at the clinic?"

"Got the call just before you came home. My eggs are fertile and your sperm is active. They're going to inject hormones in me before we leave, which will increase my production. In the middle of January they'll harvest the eggs and get fresh sperm from you.

Brett took her hand in his. "Oh Annie, that's great."

"How will we do it? We'll be back in Florida," Annie said.

"Don't worry about it, our main man, Rob, is on call. With only three of us in the plane, he can get us back to California in about five hours. Do we have an exact date?"

"Liz will coordinate it with the doctors and of

course with Samantha. She has to be ready because they'll plant at least four embryos about five to seven days after fertilization."

Brett's mouth just hung open. God, this was really going to happen. "Should I send the first payment?" he finally said.

"Do you have twenty-five thousand in your petty cash?"

"Just give me the address; I'll pop it in the mail tomorrow."

The bartender approached, "You guys want to order here or go into the dining room?"

Brett looked at Annie. "We're good here," she replied.

"Get a bunch of appetizers," Brett said.

Annie ordered the Pan Seared Crab Cakes, some Steamed Clams, and an order of Garlic Sourdough. They both nursed their drinks as they looked out the window at the airliners on final approach to the San Francisco Airport.

When the food arrived, Annie asked, "Is everything ready for Palm Beach?"

Brett dipped a piece of the bread into the clam broth and devoured a huge bite. "Pretty much. We have the estate, the office and the bank account. I've reserved the cars, and the clothier is waiting anxiously. Tomorrow we'll make the wire transfers to the Bank in Miami. I still need you to make the nail and pedicure appointments and get your ticket to New York."

Annie finished the first Crab Cake and washed

it down with the last of her Margarita.

"Do you have the phone numbers for the salons?"

"Yeah, Drake faxed me all that info. I'll give them to you tomorrow."

"I know we decided on Jan 4th for my trip. What time should I get the flight?"

"Anytime is fine. The plan doesn't change."

"Okay, I'll take care of everything after we make the wire transfers."

Brett was silent, just admiring how beautiful and radiant Annie looked. Finally he said, "Let's finish this food and drive straight home.

She gave him a grin. "Are those just bumps on your forehead, or do I see horns growing there?"

"They ain't bumps," Brett replied, as he reached for the check.

CHAPTER 27

Brett poured himself a cup of coffee and leaned over to kiss Annie. "That was special last night," he said.

"You were so ready, I was afraid we wouldn't make it to the bedroom."

He laughed, "I guess I was a little over eager."

"Just a little, but it was nice."

"Do you have your list for today?" Brett asked.

"Yes General, I have it."

"Sorry, I'm a little charged up. You know what to do; I don't have to keep telling you. I'll do my part and get the hundred and ninety wired."

"Go to the office," Annie said, "and drive Ginger nuts for a while."

Brett laughed, "I get it, you want me out of your hair today."

"Roger that," Annie replied.

Annie threw on a pair of jeans and a wool sweater. It was almost December and the mornings were getting cold. The money, $5 million, which she had received from the life insurance on J.T. was spread out through three banks. One by one she emptied each account with a wire transfer to the Miami Bank & Trust.

After leaving the third bank, she stopped at a travel agency that Brett had recommended. An eager agent invited Annie to her desk. "What can I help you with," She asked.

"I need a one way ticket to La Guardia on the fourth of January."

The agent scrolled through a screen on her computer. "Jet Blue has a pretty good fare for that day, $285. You sure you don't need a flight back? It only adds twenty-three dollars."

"Don't need it. Let's save the money."

"No problem. It leaves here at seven thirty-five and gets into La Guardia at four thirty-five New York time."

"Great, book it," Annie said, as she handed the agent her credit card.

After securing the ticket, she stopped at the only butcher shop still left in the neighborhood and bought two T-bone veal chops. She threw them in the fridge and went upstairs to the office where she looked over the fax that had been sent from Drake Caymen to Brett.

Drake had carefully spelled out Maria's beauty schedule. *The first and third Thursday of each month she has her nails done at Nails by Nadia in Palm Beach. On the second and fourth Thursday she has a pedicure at Pampered Feet also on the island. Once a month, usually the first week, she has her hair done at Sal's Salon in West Palm.*

Annie dialed the number for the nail studio. "Nails by Nadia, Joselle speaking; how may I help you?"

"Hello Joselle, I'd like to make an appointment for myself and a friend on Thursday January 5th."

"No problem, what time is good?"

"I have a friend who comes to you. I thought I'd surprise her and get an appointment at the same time. You may remember her, Maria Russ."

"Oh, I know her well. That will be so cool. Let's see, she'll be here at eleven that day."

"You have room for two more?"

"For sure, could I have the names?"

"Marcella Rojas and Carmen Diaz. We live on the island."

"Wonderful, we'll see you on the 5th of January at eleven; and don't worry I'll keep the secret."

"Thanks Joselle, see you then."

Annie made her next call. "Pampered Feet of Palm Beach," the receptionist answered.

Annie used the same scenario and secured appointments for Marcella and Carmen on Thursday, January 12th at two o'clock; the same time as Maria.

Brett came home early at three o'clock and was greeted at the door by Annie. "Good news and a big surprise," she said.

"Let's hear it."

"The money is on its way, I've got my ticket to New York, and Marcella and Carmen are set up to meet Maria."

Brett gave her a kiss. "You're the greatest. Hey, what's the big surprise?"

"Grilled veal chops for dinner."

CHAPTER 28

December 5th came up fast on Brett. His calendar read *place Chronicle ads.*

He dialed the number of advertising and circulation; it was answered by a clerk. "Are you a subscriber?" the voice asked abruptly.

"Yes, I am," responded Brett.

"Want these ads billed to your address on file? If so give it to me."

Brett was getting a little pissed with the impersonal attitude of the clerk. "That would be fine, but you might want to ask my name before you start filling in the blanks."

The clerk didn't get the sarcasm. "Name."

"Raven, 44 Geranium Lane, San Carlos."

The robot responded. "Dates and wording."

December 10th, personal section. To Long Lost Friend: *"eager to see you again. Jan. 4th at La Guardia Jet Blue terminal."*

December 11th, personal section. From Long Lost Friend: *"Bring a black briefcase. I'll take yours, you take mine."*

"That it?" the voice droned.

"That's it. Read it back."

The clerk read it back and said, "Sounds like you're sending it to yourself."

"Listen asshole; just put the ads in the paper. The rest is none of your fucking business."

"I guess some people are just unfriendly," he said. "Thank you for the ads. Goodbye."

The clerk's efficiency was apparently better than his demeanor. The ad on the 10th was perfect as well as the one on the 11th.

It was Wednesday, which meant that tomorrow night Brett would put out the garbage cans for the Friday pick up. He yelled downstairs, "Hey Annie, where is your ticket to New York?"

She yelled back, "top drawer of my desk."

Brett opened the drawer and took out the ticket which was slipped into a Jet Blue vertical envelope along with a short itinerary typed by the travel agent. He replaced the ticket but not the itinerary. All it said was:

ANNIE FRAZIER
JET BLUE FLIGHT 873-
SFO to LGA—01/04/01-

Depart—7:30 am PST-
Arrive— 4:35 pm EST-

As he had done with his previous plant, he took the sheet and rolled it in a ball, then opened it up and tore it in half lengthwise and again crosswise. He went into the garage and opened the blue recycle can. Again he tore up the junk mail, carefully placed his four pieces in the pile, spread it randomly across the top of the newspapers which were stacked to the top of the can, and closed the lid.

The next night he set his alarm for four a.m. and was pleased to spot Biff rifling through his garbage at four-thirty.

CHAPTER 29

The New Year was approaching rapidly. The day after Christmas Brett gave Rob a call. "We all set for the 2nd?"

Rob sounded excited. "Been counting the days. Should I still plan the flight for seven people with luggage?"

"I haven't had any dropouts; so let's count on that."

"Okay, I'll calculate how much fuel we can take. I'm guessing we'll have to stop twice."

"I'll leave that all up to you. You're our chief pilot."

Rob laughed. "I've come a long way since you took me on my first flight. Thanks."

"My pleasure Rob, you've made me real proud. See you at six a.m. on Monday morning."

Brett gave a call to Enrique. "Everyone still on board?" he asked.

"Everybody's looking forward to it. They think it's a vacation, but I'm thinking a little different."

"That's why you're the boss; you're smarter than everyone else. See you at six a.m. Monday."

Annie wasn't leaving with the group on the Citation; however, she drove Brett down to the San Jose airport. When they arrived at six ten, twenty minutes early, the rest of the group was already there having coffee and doughnuts in the lounge. "Wow, this is an eager group. I guess everybody's ready for adventure," Brett said.

Carmen jumped to her feet. "This is so exciting. I feel like a spy or something."

Just then, Rob came out of the flight planning office. "Head's up group. Here's our flight plan." Everyone snapped to attention. "Because we're loaded full of people and luggage, we can't fill our tanks to the top or we'll be overweight, so we'll only be carrying four hundred gallons instead of five sixty four."

"Oh, oh, is that bad?" Marcella asked.

Rob chuckled, "No, it's fine. It just means we'll have to make two stops instead of one. Depending on winds we should be getting at least four hundred miles an hour across the ground. We'll be traveling a total of twenty-five hundred miles, so I'll stop for fuel every eight or nine hundred. Including our stops, it should take less than seven hours. If we get out of here by seven, we should be in Miami by five eastern time."

"Hey, I thought we were going to Palm Beach," Carmen said.

Annie chimed in. "Don't forget, first you're going shopping for clothes in Miami."

"Whoops, how could I forget that."

Manny was looking out the window. "Hey, Rob, it's starting to rain pretty hard. Is that going to be a problem?"

"No problem, we're climbing to thirty-one thousand feet. We'll be above all this weather. Any other questions before we get going?"

Omar raised his hand and Rob pointed his index finger in Omar's direction.

"Is there a potty on board?"

"Oh, I'm glad you brought that up. There's a flush potty behind a partition in the back of the plane. If you need it, use it, but we'll be stopping every two hours and hopefully you can freshen up in a little roomier area inside the jet terminals."

"Let's get going," Enrique suggested.

Rob picked up his flight case. "Okay everyone; your bags have already been stowed in the luggage compartments. Just grab your carry-ons and let's board."

The door on the left side of the plane was open

to the ground and it created a short staircase into the plane. Enrique, Marcella, Manny and Carmen entered first and settled into the four brown and beige leather seats which faced each other in the middle of the aircraft. There was a single seat facing sideways situated behind the pilots seats, which was perfect for Omar; it offered extra leg room for him to stretch out. Brett kissed Annie goodbye, scrambled up the stairs, and took the right co-pilot seat. Rob the last one to board, secured the door shut, gave the passengers instructions for emergency evacuation, and then took his place in the left pilot seat.

Both pilots buckled their seat belts and put on the lightweight single ear headsets. Rob handed Brett a clipboard. "I planned the first leg from here to Albuquerque, which should take a little over two hours. The radios are yours; go ahead and contact Clearance Delivery and copy the instructions while I go through the start up."

Brett set in 118.0 on the number one radio. "Clearance; Citation six, eight, Charlie, Lima, ready to copy IFR clearance to Albuquerque."

The controller read the clearance to Brett, and Brett read it back to him. Rob had the engines humming by then and Brett turned in his direction. Rob gave him a thumbs up and Brett switched his other radio to 121.7. "San Jose ground; six, eight, Charlie, Lima, ready to taxi IFR to Albuquerque."

In less than five minutes the Citation was cleared for takeoff and as Rob advanced the throttles it savagely roared down the runway. When his speed reached 111 knots, 128 mph, he rotated the nose upward and trimmed the jet to climb at two thousand feet per minute. They were cleared to thirty-one thousand feet direct Fresno and then Jet airway 110 to Las Vegas. After Las Vegas they received a direct routing to Albuquerque. The weather was clear over the entire state of New Mexico, enabling Rob to touch down on the runway two hours and six minutes after leaving San Jose.

After taxiing to the Jet terminal and shutting down the engines, Rob went aft to the passenger cabin and opened the door, dropping the staircase to the ground. He turned to the passengers; "We're in Albuquerque, New Mexico. We'll be taking on fuel here, so you have twenty minutes to hit the bathrooms and freshen up. I've ordered sandwiches and drinks for our next leg, so don't buy any food. See ya in twenty."

Rob had flight planned the second leg, Albuquerque to Houston. It was the shortest of the three legs, seven hundred and forty-five statute miles, and the anticipated flight time was only an hour and forty-five minutes. Brett again handled the radios and received all the clearances allowing Rob to concentrate on his flying duties. They were airborne and leveled at thirty-three thousand, just forty-five minutes from their arrival in Albuquerque.

Rob checked their distance from Houston; a hundred and twenty miles. "I have a feeling those dark clouds below us mean IFR conditions on the ground. Go ahead and dial up the weather for the airport," he said to Brett.

Brett looked up the automated weather frequency and set 124.6 in his radio. The recording came to life. "Houston Hobby Airport Automated Weather Information Tango, one nine one three Zulu time. Wind 010 degrees at thirteen knots, gusting to twenty knots. Visibility two miles in light rain. Sky condition, eight hundred overcast. Temperature, fourteen Celsius, dew point twelve Celsius. Altimeter 29.90. Instrument approach, ILS runway one two right in use. Contact tower on 118.7. Report you have information Tango."

"You were right. It's down to eight hundred overcast and two miles," Brett said.

"That'll work," Rob responded, as the controller came on the frequency with the instructions to descend to one five thousand.

The controller kept Rob coming down until he was at four thousand feet and then turned him to a heading of one five zero and instructed him to intercept the localizer, the instrument guide needle, and cleared him to join the ILS instrument approach to runway one two. By now they were embedded in clouds and the plane was being buffeted around, so Brett began calling out the altitude for Rob every hundred feet as the Citation descended. Just as he said "eight hundred," the identifier lights at the approach end of runway one two came into view. "Got it?" Brett asked.

"Got it," Rob answered, as he put in an extra ten degrees of flaps and gently retarded the power of the engines. The runway was a safe seventy-six hundred feet long; however, Rob reversed the thrust of the engines after touchdown to shorten the roll out distance.

After shutting the engines down at the jet terminal, Rob gave the passengers an abbreviated version of his last announcement. "Sorry about the bumps, we had a little weather on our approach. We're in Houston, you know the drill. See ya back in twenty."

The last and longest leg of the trip east was from Houston to Miami, a distance of nine hundred sixty-one miles. Normally the elapsed time would be two hours and fifteen minutes; however, due to the bad weather, they had to wait twenty minutes for their instrument clearance before being cleared for takeoff.

At thirty-five thousand feet the Citation was above the weather and the ride was smooth. By the time Brett contacted Miami approach on 124.85 the weather was clear and the visibility unrestricted. Rob was cleared for a visual approach and straight in landing on runway eight right at Miami International.

It was only ten minutes after five when Rob shut the engines down in front of Landmark Aviation, an upscale Jet Center, which catered to the wealthy private and corporate jet traffic. Before the entourage exited the Citation, an employee extended a red carpet from the plane to the door of the exclusive terminal. Once inside the group waited in a VIP lounge, which was well stocked with sandwiches, sweets and soft drinks, while Brett signed for the rental cars.

CHAPTER 30

Marcella and Carmen gave Rob a big kiss on the cheek; Enrique, Manny and Omar shook his hand. "Great job," Enrique said.

Everybody else chimed in, "Really great," they echoed.

Rob smiled and said, "Hey, this isn't goodbye. I'll be waiting for you at the estate in a couple hours."

Rob headed back to the plane and the rest of the group loaded their luggage into the cars waiting outside the front door. Enrique and Marcella took possession of the black Lincoln Town Car, Manny and Carmen slipped into a black Escalade, and Brett and Omar jumped into the remaining black

Escalade.

Brett led the way and the other two vehicles followed. As Brett glanced into his rear view mirror, he couldn't keep from smiling. Enrique was slipping into character. His shiny black Lincoln was being escorted by a black Escalade in front and another in the rear; it definitely looked like a scene from "The Godfather."

In thirty-five minutes the trio of autos pulled up in front of Dolce & Gabbana. Norman had arranged to keep the store open just for Brett's group and he was waiting at the curb to greet his January pay check. "Just leave the keys in the ignitions. I'll have the cars parked for you," he said to the drivers.

As Norman escorted the group through the front doors he delivered his well-rehearsed speech. "I want to welcome all of you to Dolce & Gabbana. Doctor Raven has already filled me in on your clothing needs. My name's Norm; I'll be helping the men and my associate Elisa will be assisting the ladies."

On cue, an attractive blonde haired woman with a deep tan approached the new customers. "Hello everyone, I'm Elisa."

Brett took his cue. "Elisa, this is Mrs. Rojas and Mrs. Diaz. They're looking forward to your expertise."

Elisa shook hands with the ladies and led them off toward the rear of the store. Brett introduced Norman to Carlos Alberto Rojas and Emanuel Diaz and they were escorted to the second floor men's department.

Brett took a seat near the coffee counter and called Annie on his cell phone. "We're here," he said, after Annie had answered.

"How was the flight?"

"Flawless. That kid is really a good pilot. Made me feel like a beginner."

"Sounds like it dented your ego a little."

"Not at all, just the opposite. I'm really proud of him and it makes me feel good knowing I helped him get there."

"What time will you get to the estate?"

"It's six thirty and everyone's shopping. I'm guessing we'll get out of here in a couple hours and probably be in Palm Beach by ten."

"Is there food in the house?"

"Yeah, I gave Patricia a shopping list and she had the cupboards and fridge stocked. She wanted to be there to greet us, but I didn't want her sizing up her new tenants, so I talked her into just sending me the keys. Rob has a set and he'll be there when we arrive."

"I can't wait to join you guys."

"You'll be here soon enough. You all set for Wednesday?"

"Ready as I'll ever be."

"See you Wednesday night. I love you."

"Love you too."

It took less than two hours for Norman and Elisa to outfit the two couples. Norman had a 'go-for' handy who carried the purchases to the cars.

Each of the women had two pair of linen and two pair of silk slacks. They each had a couple sheer blouses and a couple of sleeveless ones to go with the slacks. Elisa made sure they had outfits featuring toreador pants and matching tops along with a couple cocktail dresses for the evenings. She also made sure they had matching belts and a couple pair of platform wedges and high heeled, open-toed shoes.

The men received outfits similar to the one Brett had bought two months earlier. Several pair of linen slacks with cotton short sleeved sport shirts to match. Each of them was fitted for a blue suit. Carlos' was dark blue with light pinstripes, while Manny's was less flashy with no stripes. White silk shirts and ties to match were chosen by Norman. They each received lightweight casual loafers, tan loafers, and a pair of dressy black tassel loafers.

A tailor had stayed to measure the customers and all the slacks, dresses, and suits needing alterations were scheduled to arrive late Wednesday afternoon at the estate.

There was no moon on January 2nd 2001, as the small motorcade slipped into the estate on South Ocean Boulevard without being noticed by neighbors or any passerby. The outside property lights were glowing softly and Rob had turned on lights in the main house and all three of the smaller units. As the cars made their way up the drive Marcella turned to Enrique. "Can you believe this? It looks like our own personal Ritz Carlton." Enrique just smiled; he had expected as much.

Rob swung the front doors open and greeted the entourage as they entered the main house. "Oh, my God," Carmen said. "Is this for real?"

Brett smiled and said, "Okay, Carlos and Marcella in the big master and Manny and Carmen in the smaller one. I'll take the guest house, and Omar, you're in the beach house. Rob is already unpacked in the pool house. Let's get a good night's sleep and we'll have a meeting after breakfast in the morning."

CHAPTER 31

Brett couldn't fall asleep, he was too amped up. He finally dropped off at two-thirty and slept until eight. After a shower and shave he headed to the kitchen of the main house where he found Marcella and Carmen busy preparing bacon and eggs. "Morning," Brett said.

Marcella looked up. "Good morning, coffee?"

"Please."

Carmen ran to the carafe, poured a cup and brought it to Brett. "Carmen, you don't have to wait on me. We're all on our own here."

"I can't help it. I'm so grateful to you for bringing us here. It's like I'm in a dream and I don't want to wake up."

Brett laughed. "Okay, I understand, but don't spoil me or Annie will never forgive you."

One by one the other men meandered in. The women took the bacon, eggs, fresh fruit, toast and coffee out to the terrace where they had set the table for eight. Brett looked at the setting. "Hey, you set it for an extra person."

Marcella looked up. "Annie belongs with us, so we'll set an empty place until she gets here. When will that be?"

Brett was touched. "Tomorrow night," he said.

Everyone was famished from their long day yesterday. They emptied the breakfast platters in two minutes and each of their plates was cleaned in five. Enrique poured himself another cup of coffee and spoke. "Okay, Brett, let's hear what's next."

"Today and tomorrow are get ready days. The women can get a feel for the house and relax at the pool or the beach. Enrique, or Carlos Alberto I should say, will establish a little office in the library, which will look as if he's doing big business out of it. I'll take Manny to his new office downtown and get him settled in. Rob, you can do whatever you want."

"How about me?" Omar asked.

"Oh yeah, Omar, you can clean your gun." Everyone, including Omar, broke out laughing.

"When does the real work start?" Manny asked.

"Thursday morning at eleven a.m. Marcella and Carmen have nail appointments at Nails by Nadia. Dress to impress. You're going to start up your friendship with Maria."

"What should we talk about?" Marcella asked.

"Talk a lot about yourselves and a lot about the estate and a lot about how much money you have. By the end of the appointment, I want Marcella to invite Carmen and her husband and Maria and her husband to the estate for cocktails on Saturday evening."

"What if she doesn't want to come?" Carmen asked.

"Don't worry, she will." Brett replied. "Saturday night, Carlos and Manny will go to work on Antonio. We'll rehearse it on Saturday morning. Omar, whenever Alberto and Marcella have guests, you'll be at the gate to let them in. Make sure that gun shows through your blue blazer. Rob, get ready for a flight to the Bahamas in a few weeks."

CHAPTER 32

Jet Blue flight 873 was delayed an hour and fifteen minutes. Annie wasn't concerned; she knew the people waiting for her at La Guardia would be constantly checking the arrival screen.It was six fifteen by the time the exit line started to depart the Boeing 737 in New York.

As she came through the jetway, Annie gave a quick scan of the lobby. There were about twenty people waiting for friends and relatives, and another fifty or sixty waiting to board at an adjacent gate. About fifty feet ahead and to her right she spotted Biff, a physique which was difficult to hide, standing next to a man in a blue suit. She didn't make eye contact and glanced to her left where other departing passengers were making their way toward the baggage area. A good looking guy about six two with blond hair, dressed in jeans and a leather jacket, caught her eye and nodded ever so slightly as he placed his black briefcase on the carpet.

Annie followed the other passengers until she was abreast of the man and then she broke ranks and headed straight to him. She placed her own black briefcase next to his and said a few words before she walked away and entered the ladies room.

When she emerged from the bathroom, the blond stranger was surrounded by Biff and the guy in the Blue suit. As she got closer she could see that the guy in the suit had a good build and wore horn rimmed glasses. She wondered if he had a superman outfit under his shirt. "Excuse me, that's my briefcase," she said as she reached toward the ground.

"Is your name Annie Talbot?" the suit asked.

"It was; I go by Frazier now. Who are you?"

The suit reached into his pocket and produced a brown leather folding wallet, flipped it open exposing a badge, and said, "I'm special agent Landon, Federal Bureau of Investigation, Fraud Division."

"What does that have to do with me?" Annie said.

"I have reason to believe you met this man here to receive and transport stolen money across state lines."

"That's preposterous."

The agent turned to the blond man. "If I'm not mistaken, your name is J.T. Talbot."

The man laughed. "Unfortunately you are mistaken."

"May I see your I.D.?" The agent smirked.

The blond pulled out a passport and handed it to the agent. The agent reached into his pocket, brought out a photograph, and compared it to the passport and then to the man. He didn't look happy and shot a dirty look in Biff's direction. "Why did you give this man your briefcase?" he asked Annie.

"I didn't give it to him; I asked if he could watch it while I was in the bathroom."

"Why wouldn't you take it with you?"

"Have you seen the floors in the stalls? I really don't like urine on my possessions, especially a brand new leather case."

"Why would you trust this man?"

"He didn't look like a briefcase napper to me."

"I'd like permission to examine both of your briefcases."

"For what reason?" Annie asked.

"Mr. Erskine, here, has reasonable cause to believe there's a million dollars in one of those cases."

"The reasonable cause you're talking about was probably extracted from my garbage can. That's the last place I saw Mr. Erskine."

The agent winced as he gave another disparaging

glance toward Biff. "May I have permission or not?"

The blond guy spoke up. "I think you're harassing this woman, and frankly you're also harassing me."

"Sir, I can actually arrest both of you and inspect the briefcases after I book you."

"I want to see your badge again," the guy said.

The agent reached in his pocket and put the badge up where it was in plain view. The blond guy pulled a pen and paper out of his jacket and carefully wrote down the name of the agent and the number of the badge. "Okay, you can look in my case, but you're going to be disappointed, and your boss is going to hear from my lawyer tomorrow morning."

The agent had heard this threat many times before when he had guilty suspects, but this time he sensed he wasn't in a position of strength. "Ma'am, sir, I apologize for this inconvenience. If you just allow me to open the cases and I find Mr. Erskine is misinformed, we can all go on our separate ways,"

"Open it," Annie said.

"Be my guest," the guy added.

The agent picked up the first case. "Whose is this?' he asked.

"That's mine," Annie responded.

Landon unzipped the top of the case and reached in. He pulled out two Tampons, a peanut butter sandwich and a magazine about breastfeeding newborns. He quickly replaced the items and picked up the other briefcase. He hurriedly opened it and it produced two girlie magazines, a bible, and six packs of chewing gum. His face turned crimson and he said softly, "Sorry, folks, you're free to go."

Annie snatched the case and swung it around with such force it hit the agent in the groin as she walked off. The blond guy picked up his and said, "Go catch some bad guys, asshole." As he walked away he saw the blue suit poking his finger into the chest of Biff Erskine.

Annie left the terminal, hailed a cab and jumped in through the right rear door. Just then the left door opened and the blond guy hopped in beside her. "Can you take us to the General Aviation Terminal?" he said to the driver. "I know it's a small fare, but I'll throw in an extra twenty."

As the cab pulled away from the curb, Annie turned toward the man. "Drake Caymen, I'm so happy to finally meet you. Brett said you had brown hair."

"Annie it's my pleasure, and yes, I do, but I dyed it for today's performance"

Drake gave the cabbie thirty-two dollars and he and Annie entered the terminal used by the private jets.

Brett was waiting inside and gave Annie a big hug. "Hey, guys, how did it go?"

"Perfect," Drake said. "Annie should be an actress. It'll be a long time before the FBI will believe anything Biff tells them again."

Just then Rob walked out of the pilot's lounge. "I filed a flight plan to Miami so we can drop off

Drake. Everyone ready to head for Florida?"

Annie and Drake picked up their cases. "Let's go," Annie said, looking forward to a nap in one of the soft leather seats of the Citation.

CHAPTER 33

When Marcella and Carmen walked into the kitchen on Thursday morning, they were met with the smell of biscuits baking in the oven. "I'm making you a special breakfast for your first day at work," Annie looked up and said.

Both women were ecstatic and rushed to give her a hug. "Annie, you're here," Carmen exclaimed.

"We've missed you," Marcella added.

"Brett told me how sweet you guys were. Thanks," she said, as she hugged them back.

One by one the rest of the crew staggered in, each greeting Annie with a kiss or hug.

Annie threw four diced green peppers along with eight sliced up Italian sausages into an extra-large frying pan coated with olive oil. When the meat and peppers were brown and sizzling, she covered them with a dozen and a half scrambled eggs and mixed everything together. She found a huge platter in the cabinet and spooned the mixture onto it, lining the fresh biscuits up along the edges. "Let's eat," she said as she headed for the outdoor terrace.

Brett didn't spend a lot of time giving instructions. Both women knew their assignments and he was confident they could complete them. When breakfast was over he simply said, "Break a leg."

Marcella pulled the Escalade up in front of the nail studio and gave the keys to the parking attendant who had already opened the door for Carmen. Both women looked exquisite. Each wore an outfit with toreador pants; Marcella with a sleeveless blouse to match and Carmen with a sheer silk blouse which displayed her two most obvious attributes. Marcella chose her pair of high heeled open toed shoes and Carmen wore her platform wedges. Both women had on almost a pound of jewelry.

After checking in with the receptionist, they were escorted to the working area. There were six stations positioned in the shape of a horseshoe with the customers on the outside and the technicians on the inside facing them. It was the perfect arrangement for conversation.

They both spotted Maria immediately. She

was seated in the second chair on the left and as described, tall, blonde and very attractive. Marcella was directed to the fourth chair and Carmen to the fifth. Unfortunately, in order to talk to Maria they would have to talk past the woman in chair number three.

As soon as the technicians began their work, Marcella directed conversation toward chair number three. "Hello, I'm Marcella, this is my friend Carmen."

"Oh, hello, I'm Gloria and this is Maria next to me."

Maria waved and said, "Nice to meet you."

They began with small talk about nails, the salon, and where to buy the best frozen yogurt. Then Maria asked, "Do you live on the island or in West Palm?"

Marcella jumped on the opening. "I live on South Ocean. Carmen lives about a mile away."

"Those are beautiful homes on the Boulevard. How long have you been there?" Maria asked.

"A couple years, but we travel a lot so we're not here all the time. How long have you lived here Carmen?"

"We've been here a long time. Marcella's husband is a client of my husband."

"What do your husbands do?" Maria asked.

"My husband Emanuel is a loan broker and Carlos Alberto, Marcella's husband, is an importer."

"How interesting, what does Carlos import?" Maria asked Marcella.

"I really don't know and I don't ask. Whatever it is, it pays for a lot of stuff."

Gloria laughed and entered in. "How much property do you own on South Ocean?"

"I think about two acres, Carlos likes privacy. He doesn't want neighbors close by."

"Is it all oceanfront?" Maria asked, already impressed with the address.

Carmen joined in. "It is, and you should see their layout. It's really not a house, it's an estate. There's like four houses on the property."

Marcella waved her hand in the air. "It's no big deal."

"Sounds lovely," Maria said.

"Where do you guys live?" Carmen asked.

"I'm in West Palm. Where are you Gloria?" Maria asked.

"West Palm also."

By eleven forty-five the polish was almost dry on the ladies nails and Gloria and Maria were duly impressed with the wealth exhibited by Marcella and Carmen, especially Marcella.

All four women walked to the reception desk together, paid their bills and left their tips. Marcella knew this was her last chance to deliver the invite, but Gloria was still in the mix; she had to make her move and went ahead anyway. "Hey, would you two like to join us with your husbands this Saturday night? Carmen and Manny are coming over for cocktails and a light supper."

Both women lit up. It wasn't every day you

get an invitation to an estate on South Ocean Boulevard.

"I'm sure we could make it," Maria answered.

"I'll have to check with my husband," Gloria responded. "Could I call you this afternoon?"

"Sure," Marcella said. "Why don't I give both of you my number." She pulled out two Carlos Alberto Rojas business cards and jotted her cell phone number on the back of them. "Let's plan on seven o'clock. Oh, and just very Palm Beach casual, no ties for the guys."

They all shook hands as their cars were delivered. "Gloria, I'll wait for your call. Maria, we'll plan on you for sure," Marcella said, as she tipped the attendant with a ten dollar bill.

Everyone was trying to be nonchalant, but in truth, all were waiting anxiously for the women to return. "I think they're here," Rob exclaimed.

Marcella and Carmen emerged through the entryway and into the living room where the entire group was assembled. "Good news?" Brett asked.

"Better than good, fabulous!" Marcella responded.

"You should have seen Marcella," Carmen added. "The two women were salivating all over their nail polish."

"What do you mean two women?" Brett asked.

"Well that was the only glitch. We couldn't get Maria alone, so I had to invite both Maria and this gal Gloria. She's only a maybe, but if she responds that she's coming, you'll have to work around her and her husband." Marcella said.

Brett gave each of the women a big cheek kiss. "That's fine; the main thing is that Maria and Antonio are coming. You guys did great. Hey Rob, make yourself useful and mix a pitcher of Martinis."

"Roger that," Rob said as he headed for the liquor cabinet.

CHAPTER 34

Unfortunately Gloria accepted the invitation, so in preparation for Saturday night, Annie met with a caterer and arranged a dinner for eight instead of six.

Omar positioned himself at the gate to the property dressed in jeans, a tee shirt, and a tight blue blazer which accentuated the bulge in the breast pocket. Carlos and Manny dressed in linen slacks and silk sport shirts. Marcella and Carmen wore just the opposite; silk slacks and linen blouses. Rob, Brett and Annie left the property at six o'clock and headed to West Palm for dinner and a movie.

A Mercedes two door carrying Maria and Antonio approached the gate a couple minutes before seven and Omar lumbered up to the driver's window. "Good evening sir, may I have your name?"

"Antonio and Maria Russ," the driver answered.

Omar carried a clipboard and ran his finger down the paper which was attached to the top. He nodded his head, and then he dialed in a code and the gate opened. "Thank you, Mr. Russ," he said. "Just park your car in front of the main residence."

As the gate closed on the Mercedes, a Lexus 430 pulled up. Again Omar asked their name. "Pete and Gloria Henson," the driver responded. Omar checked his board, opened the gate, and directed them to follow the Mercedes.

Marcella and Carlos were at the front entrance as the two cars arrived on the circular drive to the residence. "Welcome, welcome," Carlos said as he kissed the top of each woman's right hand. "I'm Carlos and this is Marcella."

"Hello again," Marcella said to Maria and Gloria. "I'm so glad you were able to join us." "Antonio and Maria," the tall blond man said, while extending his hand to Carlos.

"Pete and Gloria," the shorter man added. "Thanks for the invitation."

Everyone shook hands and then Carlos led the delegation through the house and onto the terrace where the guests were introduced to Manny and Carmen.

The caterer had provided a bartender who approached the group and took drink orders. As soon as the drinks arrived the women disappeared into the house for a tour while the men huddled around the Tuna Tartare. "So how do you guys stay busy?" Carlos asked.

"I'm a CPA in West Palm," Pete answered.

"How about you Antonio?"

"Actually, I'm retired. We just moved to Florida about three months ago."

"I'm impressed," Manny said. "You're still a young guy."

"Got lucky," Antonio answered. "Maria told me you're a loan broker. Where do you place your money?"

"You a financial guy?" Manny asked.

"Yeah, I used to be a planner."

"I figured you were. Right now I work exclusively with two clients; Carlos Alberto is one of them."

"You're an importer?" Pete asked Carlos.

"Yeah, stuff coming in from South America mostly."

"So how does Manny fit in?" Antonio asked.

Manny took the lead. "When Carlos has a big shipment coming in, I arrange financing for its payment. Then he sells the product, pays my investors and my commission, and takes the rest as profit. Everybody wins."

"What exactly do you import?" Pete asked Carlos.

"Is this a good area for CPA's?" Carlos asked Pete, ignoring the previous question.

The diversion wasn't lost on Antonio, but Pete

seemed to like talking about himself and didn't mind the change of subject. "Yes, yes, very good." He took three cards from his breast pocket and handed them out to the men. "If you need any services, give me a call."

Just then the women returned from their tour of the property. "Antonio, you have to see this place. Their pool house is the size of our condo." Maria said.

"Would you like a tour? Carlos asked.

"Sure," Antonio answered. "You, Pete?"

"Great," Pete responded.

Carlos led the two men through the main residence, making sure he showed them his office. Then he passed by the outside of the guest house, pool house and beach house, and finally returned them to the terrace where the ladies were making small talk.

"Very impressive," Antonio said. "Manny, do you have a spread like this?"

Manny smiled. "I live on the poor side of the island."

Pete joined in. "There is no poor side to this island." Everybody laughed.

The caterers served a very elegant dinner during which Manny kept his eyes on Antonio. He noticed him sizing up Carlos and then Omar, who had returned from the gate and was positioned in the corner of the room like a guard dog. Occasionally he would peruse the room and take in the opulent surroundings. Manny was sure he saw him wink at Maria.

After dinner everyone drifted onto the terrace where Carlos had the bartender bring a bottle of fifty year old Port, which he served to the guests. He lifted his glass and made a toast. "To our new friends, Antonio, Maria, Pete, and Gloria." Everyone touched their glasses together.

At eleven o'clock the guests began their exit toward the front door. Marcella caught Maria and asked, "Where do you get your pedicures? Your toes are magnificent."

"I go to Pampered Feet here on the island. As a matter of fact I have an appointment this coming Thursday at two o'clock."

"Would you mind if I used your name. Maybe Carmen and I could meet up with you there."

"Oh, go right ahead, it would be great if you could; and thanks so much for having us tonight. We had a wonderful time."

Manny was able to separate Antonio from the group. "Antonio, any chance you could drop by my office? I'd like to exchange some ideas with you. I love talking to financial guys."

"Anytime," he answered.

Manny discreetly slipped him one of his business cards. "How about Monday around eleven-thirty. Maybe we can have lunch afterward."

"Great, I'll be there."

Fifteen minutes after the two cars left through the gate, a black Escalade eased onto the property and Brett, Annie and Rob joined the group on the terrace.

"How'd it play out?" Brett asked.

Everybody had a blank expression.

"What?" Brett asked.

The entire group broke out laughing. "It went perfect," Enrique said.

CHAPTER 35

Brett called for a breakfast meeting on Monday morning. By nine o'clock the entire group had assembled and was working on their second cup of coffee. "Let's review the schedule for the upcoming week," Brett said.

Manny spoke first. "I'm meeting with Antonio at eleven-thirty today. We'll get acquainted."

"Great," Brett said. "Who else has something going this week?"

"Carmen and I have appointments for pedicures at the same time as Maria on Thursday," Marcella added.

"Good, prime her for a trip to the Bahamas."

"Got it," Marcella said.

"I can't wait for that trip. It sounds so exciting," Carmen added.

Brett couldn't help but chuckle every time Carmen joined in. "That will be it for this week. Annie and I have to go back to California for a few days. Rob is flying us to San Jose tomorrow morning."

There were startled looks on several faces. "Is something wrong?" Enrique asked.

"No, but I think it's time to share some personal information with you."

Annie spoke up. "We're going to have a baby."

"Annie, you told Carmen and me that you couldn't get pregnant." Marcella said.

"Actually, I'm not. A surrogate is getting my eggs and Brett's sperm and she'll carry the baby or babies. We're headed back for donor's day this Wednesday."

"That is so far out," Carmen said, as she went to Annie and gave her a hug.

"Anyone else need to get back to California?" Brett asked. There were no takers. "Okay then, we'll be back on Thursday night. Enrique will run the show while we're gone. That good with you Enrique?"

"No problem," he answered.

Manny arrived at his office before eleven, told the receptionist to buzz him when Antonio showed up, and then sat down at his desk where he spread out file folders and papers all over the working area.

At eleven-thirty sharp the intercom buzzed. "What is it, Francene?"

"Mr. Russ is here to see you, Mr. Diaz."

"Show him in please."

Francene gave a short knock on the door, then opened it for Antonio as Manny came around from the back of his desk. "Antonio, you're right on time. Let's go into the conference room and have a cup of coffee."

"How would you like it?" Francene asked Antonio.

"Just black, thanks."

"Mr. Diaz?"

"Same."

The conference room was used by all the businesses who rented space in the suite and was therefore very spacious and very well appointed. Manny took a seat at the head of the long oak table and Antonio settled into a leather swivel chair right next to him.

"So, Antonio, what sort of financial planning did you used to do?"

"Usual stuff, short and long range investments, insurance."

"You must have had a big hit to get out so early."

"Yeah, I did. Sometimes you get lucky in that business."

"Was it all clean and tidy?"

Antonio smiled. "Sometimes the wash comes out a little dirty." He quickly changed the subject. "How do you get by with only two clients?" He asked.

"Actually it's more like one client, Carlos. I help the other guy as a favor."

"So all your income comes from Carlos? I don't want to pry, but what exactly does he import?"

Manny took a sip from his coffee and didn't say a word.

Antonio knew right away he shouldn't have asked that question. "I'm sorry, it's really none of my business," he said.

"No, no, it's all right. It's pretty private and sometimes our wash comes out a little dirty also; but when Carlos has a deal, he has a big deal. When he needs money, I usually have to raise anywhere from twenty million to over a hundred."

"Wow that is big. I think I get the idea; you don't have to spell it out. Does Omar always follow him around like he did Saturday night?"

"Yeah, that's what he's paid for. A guy tried to assassinate Carlos a couple years ago. Ever since then he's had a bodyguard twenty-four seven. Omar actually lives in the beach house on the property."

"How in the hell are you able to raise so much money for his deals?"

"I think you've figured out by now that conventional sources of money aren't available to Carlos. He's willing to give a huge return over a short period of time to his investors. They know he's working in the shadows, but they don't ask questions and just take the returns."

Antonio eyes opened a little wider. "What kind of returns are you talking about?"

"A hundred percent for a month or two."

Antonio spilled his coffee all over the table. Manny grabbed some paper towels and mopped it up. "Sorry," Antonio said. "But, did you say a hundred percent?"

"I know that sounds impossible, but when Carlos needs the money, he needs it fast. He doubles the investor's money and picks up four times that amount for himself."

"Unbelievable," Antonio uttered.

Manny went away from the money. "Did you say the other night that you were from California?"

Antonio gave it some thought. "Well, I was there for a while, but I spent a lot of time in the Midwest also. That's where I met Maria."

"What brought you to Florida?"

"Seems like a good place to retire. Weather is warm and there's no state income tax. I get the idea from your last name you're from Cuba. What brought you here?"

Manny smiled. "Yeah I'm from Havana. My parents escaped with the family when I was just a kid. I got into loan brokering when I was about twenty-five and a guy introduced me to Carlos a couple years later. That was my big break."

"Carlos is from Cuba also?"

"No, no, he's actually from Colombia. That's

where all his contacts are."

Antonio didn't want to overstep his bounds again so he changed the subject. "Maria and I really enjoyed Saturday night, but I got the feeling Pete and Gloria were out of their element."

"Yeah, well the girls all had their nails done together. Marcella is like that. She's very generous and she'll invite people over at the drop of a hat. I know she and Carlos really liked you guys, but I doubt if Ralph and Gloria will be invited back."

"Well, we also enjoyed being with them and with you and Carmen. That's quite a spread they have."

"It's somethin' else isn't it? I think he paid about ten mill a few years ago and now I'm guessing it's almost worth twice that."

Antonio let out a deep breath. "Some people have the golden touch."

Manny looked at his watch. "Hey, it's almost twelve-thirty. Let's grab a bite, lunch is on me."

"I won't argue with that," Antonio said, following Manny toward the door.

CHAPTER 36

The trip back to San Jose didn't take as long as the trip out to Miami. Although the winds moving from west to east were less favorable, the Citation was very light with only three people and no luggage, and therefore only one stop was necessary, in San Antonio Texas. Brett and Annie were back in their townhouse by 1 p.m. California time.

Annie had been injected with hormones just prior to her trip to New York, and she had been taking other oral medications to stimulate the production of eggs the entire time she was in Palm Beach. January 11th was established as the optimum day in her cycle to harvest eggs and a surgery slot was pre-scheduled for 9 a.m. at Saint Francis Hospital in downtown San Francisco.

They arrived at the hospital just before eight on Wednesday morning. Annie had been given the choice of general anesthesia or conscious sedation for the procedure and she opted for the sedation. She was wheeled into the operating room at ten after nine. While Annie was in the O.R., Brett was given a private room where he delivered fresh semen into a sterile container.

Annie was in the recovery room by ten fifteen and was alert by ten forty-five when the doctor joined her and Brett. "Everything went fine," he said. "I managed to extract eight eggs."

"Where are they now?" Annie asked.

"Believe it or not, your eggs are in the laboratory and are being fertilized by Brett's sperm as we speak."

"Unbelievable," Brett said. "How many embryos are you expecting?"

"We took eight eggs from Annie. We'll fertilize all of them and hopefully we'll get at least six embryos."

Annie's eyes opened wide. "Six? I don't think we can handle six kids at once."

The Doc gave a little chuckle. "Don't worry, you won't have six children. If we get six good embryos, we'll plant four into Samantha's uterus. If we're lucky, one will take."

"What do you do with the two you don't plant?" Brett asked.

"We'll freeze them for now, but if we don't need them for a 2nd try, the two of you will have to decide if they get destroyed or donated to another couple. You should start giving some thought to the issue. It becomes a difficult decision when you have to make it."

Annie and Brett were quiet. They hadn't given any thought to the moral and ethical decisions they would have to make after the process was over. Finally Annie changed gears and asked, "When will Samantha receive the embryos?"

"I'm guessing in five days."

"And when will we know if any take?"

"We'll do a pregnancy test in two weeks. If it's positive, we'll wait four more weeks for an ultrasound to determine how many we have."

Brett and Annie became very introspective and the doctor sensed it was time to leave. "Any more questions?" he asked.

They looked at each other and just smiled. "Guess not," Brett said.

"Okay then. You have a visitor, I'll show her in."

The doctor went out to the reception room and returned accompanied by Samantha. "I'll leave the three of you together," he said as he left the room.

Samantha gave Annie a hug and said, "I'm ready. The doc said five days."

All of a sudden Brett realized they would be back in Florida. "Samantha, do you want us here that day? We may be out of the state."

"Oh, that's okay. I've been through this before and it's not a very big deal. The action starts after we get one growing in there."

"You sure?" Annie asked. "I can stay on and join Brett later."

"No, really. I'd love you here for the ultrasound though, when we know how many."

"For sure," Brett said. "We'll be here."

Annie was a little sore from the previous day's procedure and was still in bed when Brett crawled out on Thursday morning. "Can I bring you some breakfast?" He asked.

"Maybe just toast and coffee. Mind if I stay in bed for a while?"

"That's fine; I'll bring it up on a tray. You feel good enough for the trip back this afternoon?"

"I'm fine, just a little sore and tired. I think I'm a little overwhelmed by it all."

"I know what you mean. Any regrets?"

"None." She answered. "You?"

"None whatsoever."

Brett brought the tray up to Annie. "You sure you want to go today? We can postpone it a day."

"I really miss the girls. I haven't had any close women friends in quite a while. I want to get back. What do you have to do before we leave?"

"I'm going to run up to the city for a short meeting with that guy Ralph Phillips from

Connecticut Mutual Life, then I have to check in with Ginger. She'll kill me if I don't. What time should I tell Rob?"

Annie finished her toast. "Your call, I'll just relax here this morning."

"How about three? We'll still get in at a reasonable hour."

"Gimme a kiss and get going," Annie said.

Brett planted one on her lips. "See you after lunch," he said, as he gathered up the tray.

Brett was back from San Francisco by eleven-thirty and walked into his office through the side entrance where Ginger could spot him immediately. She jumped up and gave him a hug.

"Any bullet holes?" she asked as she patted him down.

"Still in one piece," Brett said, as he gave her a hug back. "Let's catch up on things in my office."

Ginger took her usual position in Brett's lounger and he sat in his desk chair. "Any problems?" he asked.

"Nothing out of the usual, except for your friend Biff, who just won't give up."

"What do you mean?"

Ginger rolled her eyes. "Well, a couple days after you left, he came in looking angry and insisted I tell him where you had gone."

"What did you tell him?"

"Told him I didn't know and even if I did, I wouldn't tell him."

Brett laughed. "I bet he was happy to hear that."

"He walked out and slammed the door. The next day I get a call from an unidentified friend of yours who has a family emergency and wants to know how to get a hold of you."

"What did you say?"

"I told him you were in Turkmenistan and there were no phones there."

Brett cracked up. "Was he happy?"

"Said, 'Fuck you, lady,' and hung up."

Brett was still laughing. "How's John Gruber doing with my patients?"

"He's never worked so hard in his life. I saw he was really dragging so I lightened up his schedule. I forget he just got out of school."

"Is he okay with it?"

"Actually, he's very happy. With what you're paying him, he's able to keep his little practice down the street going. I feel sorry for him when you come back and he's out of a job."

"Maybe we can keep him on. I'll talk to you about it when I get back."

"When might that be?" Ginger asked.

"Probably four or five weeks. By the way we're almost pregnant."

Ginger clasped her hands together and rested her chin on them. "That's so great. I assume this is the reason you're back here."

"Yeah, the eggs were fertilized yesterday, and if we're lucky Samantha will be pregnant in four or five days."

"How's Annie?"

"A little sore, but happy."

"I'm really excited for the two of you. Is a marriage in the near future or is the baby going to have multiple last names?"

Brett frowned. "I promised Annie I wouldn't push her"

Ginger got up and gave Brett a hug. "Give Annie my best and call me once in a while rather than just showing up."

"Yes, mother," Brett said, while hugging her back.

CHAPTER 37

The weather en route to San Antonio was clear and Rob had the plane on the ground less than three hours after they had departed San Jose. The leg from there to West Palm Beach was bumpy, but nothing significant enough to slow them up. They landed at twelve-thirty a.m. and were back at the estate and in their beds by one-fifteen.

Brett and Annie staggered into breakfast at ten after nine and were greeted by the entourage. "How was the trip?" Carmen excitedly asked.

"A little bumpy," Annie replied.

Marcella interrupted. "She didn't mean that. Did they get the eggs?"

Annie smiled. "Oh, sorry. Yes, they took eight

and are hoping for at least six embryos."

Annie saw a look of shock on everyone's face. "It's not what it sounds like. Six embryos means four implants and hopefully one child. Could be more, but not likely more than two."

Enrique, who was often stingy with his affections, came over and kissed Annie on the forehead. "We're all praying for you," he said. Brett was sure he saw a tear in Enrique's eye.

Marcella and Carmen wouldn't let Annie help with breakfast and forced her to sit while they made a fresh pot of coffee and some breakfast burritos. Brett and Annie scarfed down their meal while the others, who had already eaten, sipped coffee and waited for Brett to ask for a report. It didn't take long. "So how did the pedicure appointment go?" He asked.

"Just like a man," Carmen said. "Didn't even look at the beautiful job Soo Lin did on our toes."

"Sorry," Brett said. "Let's take a look."

Carmen put her right foot on the table next to a piece of bell pepper that Brett had discarded from his burrito. "Ta, da," she said, as she spread her arms apart as if she were catching a touchdown pass.

"Beautiful," Brett said. "By the way, how did the discussion with Maria go?"

"Went well," Marcella said. "We all sat next to each other and went out for a drink afterward. Actually, we got a little plastered."

"That's an understatement," Manny said.

"Anyway, we talked about clothes, jewelry, vacation spots, anything that costs a lot of money."

"Pick up any gems?"

"Yeah, after the second Martini, Maria let slip that Antonio had put all his new found money into short term bonds until he decides on long term investments."

"Good work," Brett said. "Any idea where his bonds are?"

Carmen joined in. "Ever hear of a place called Marble Lunch?"

Everyone cracked up. "I think you mean Merrill Lynch," Enrique said.

"Whatever," Carmen said. "Who can understand anything after a couple Martinis anyway?"

Marcella noticed all the coffee cups were dry and reached to the counter where she grabbed the pot and filled the cups. "Did you get to the Bahamas trip?" Brett asked.

"Sure did," Marcella replied. "Told her Carlos had invited Carmen and Manny to fly with us over to Nassau for some fun and gambling."

"She wanted to know what airlines fly there. I was quick to say we're going in Carlos' jet," Carmen added. "Then Marcella said, 'hey maybe you guys would like to come along.'"

"How did she react?' Brett asked.

"I think she shit in her pants, she was so excited," Carmen giggled.

The guys were almost rolling on the floor. "This is better than a TV soap opera," Enrique said.

"Like you've ever watched one," Marcella replied sarcastically.

"So how did you leave it?" Annie asked.

"Told her to ask Antonio and I'd give her a call in a couple days."

"That's perfect, Brett said. "Today's Friday. Let them stand by the phone until Sunday; then call and give them the formal invite and the details."

"What are the details?" Marcella asked.

Brett laughed. "Oh, yeah, forgot about that. Okay, the trip is planned for next Friday the 20th. You'll meet them at the West Palm General Aviation Terminal at noon, where Carlos' pilot will have the jet waiting. Tell them Carlos has reserved the rooms and the weekend is on him."

"What if they want to pay for themselves?"

"I doubt that they will."

Manny interrupted. "Hey, how will that work? Antonio Russ is a phony name; He won't have a passport. Come to think of it, we have phony names also."

"I was thinking about that," Brett said. "You guys will use your own names and passports. Antonio won't see the manifest, Rob's in charge of that. Antonio will really want to take this trip and he'll probably use his old J.T. Talbot passport. He'll want to stay away from Carlos and work around it. I bet he'll be the last one in line through customs."

"What if he doesn't want to take the chance?" Enrique asked.

"Then I'll just have to think of something else,

but I really want him on that jet. He loves airplanes and flying in this one is like going to airplane heaven. It's going to be hard for him to pass it up."

There was nothing to do until Sunday, so everyone sat out at the pool or on the beach. Annie and Rob were the only ones in the group who didn't have dark complexions; they stayed under umbrellas while the others soaked in the sun and deepened their tans.

On Sunday Marcella waited until after noon and gave Maria a call. "Hi, sorry I'm so late getting back. I talked to Carlos and he wants you guys to come along and he reserved rooms for everyone. We're meeting at the airport in West Palm at noon on Friday. By the way, Carlos is picking up the tab for the entire weekend."

Maria sounded down. "Antonio doesn't know if he can make it."

"Oh, that's too bad," Marcella said. "Didn't you say Antonio used to fly his own plane?"

"Yes, he did."

"I talked to Rob, our pilot. He said Antonio could co-pilot and maybe fly a little on the trip. Too bad he'll miss out."

"Maria was silent for a moment then said, "Let me talk to him again. Can I get back to you later this afternoon?"

"Sure, try to talk him into it. We're going to have a great time."

Rob was barbequing hamburgers for lunch while the others silently nursed Mai Tai's on the terrace waiting for the phone to ring. Just as lunch was being served, Marcella's cell phone buzzed. "Oh, hi, Maria, any good news?" She waited for a response, and then said, "Is he positive? Sure, sure. Any other questions I could answer? Okay, that's fine." Then she hung up.

Everyone was grim. "Bad news?" Brett asked.

"Marcella winked at Brett. "They'll meet us at the airport at noon."

CHAPTER 38

Tuesday morning everyone except Omar was finishing breakfast when he came out on the terrace. "Brett, I think we have a visitor," he said.

"What visitor?"

"There's a guy down the street in a white Ford Fairlane who looks like he's watchin' the gate. At first I thought he was a cop so I casually walked by his car. This guy looks private dick to me."

"Is he a fat guy with a buzz cut?" Brett asked.

"Yeah, has a scar on his face like mine, only smaller."

"That's Biff Erskine, the guy who's trying to beat us to the money."

"How do we handle him?" Annie asked. "We

never thought he'd get this far."

"He's an ex-military hard ass," Brett said. "We're goin' to have to get him out of Florida."

"I know that look," Enrique said. "You've got an idea."

"This guy only responds to hard ball. Omar, walk the street again, only this time jump in the right seat of the Fairlane. Show him some metal and bring him in through the gate."

Omar was only gone five minutes before the White Ford came up the drive and parked in front of the main house. Brett and Manny were waiting and Manny went to help. He jerked Biff out of the car and both he and Omar pushed him against the front fender. Omar held him while Manny patted him down. He removed a pair of handcuffs off Biff's belt and a Beretta 9mm from an ankle holster.

"You shouldn't have come here," Brett said. "Now it's going to get ugly having to deal with you."

"You don't scare me, you little dentist prick," Biff responded.

"Shut your fuckin' mouth asshole," Omar said, as hc landed a right cross across Biff's left cheek.

Biff fell to his knees and put his hand to his face feeling for the source of the blood that was running down his neck.

Manny pulled him to his feet and used Biff's own handcuffs to lock his hands behind his back. "Where should we put him?" Manny asked.

"Cuff him to the bed in the beach house," Brett

replied, as he turned and went into the main house.

Ft. Lauderdale is forty-five miles south of Palm Beach and twenty-three miles north of Miami. Brett thumbed through the yellow pages until he found the name, Custom Boat Rental at Pier 66. "I need a small boat for twenty-four hours to do some off shore fishing. What's available?"

"We have a couple small Boston Whalers. When do you want it?"

"We'd like to pick it up this afternoon and do some fishing tomorrow. What's the cost?"

"You could pick it up this afternoon around four; it runs $300 a day plus gas."

"Sounds good, reserve it for me. My name's Manny."

"Okay Manny. See you this afternoon."

Brett asked Manny and Omar to meet him on the terrace. "How's our guy doing?" he asked.

"He has a black eye and he's pretty swollen. I brought him a sandwich and let him use the John. He's still trying to be a tough guy." Manny replied.

"I figured as much. We're going to really have to scare the shit out of him to break him. Omar, go down to a building supply store in West Palm and pick up two fifty pound cement foundation blocks. Make sure they have some sort of hook and pick up twenty feet of chain to attach to them. Manny, you keep an eye on Biff."

Omar had to shop several supply stores, but finally found what Brett had asked for. He loaded the supplies into the trunk of the Fairlane. At three o'clock Manny marched Biff, still restrained by handcuffs, to the car and pushed him into the back seat. He took a roll of duct tape and wrapped it around Biffs ankles. "You gonna keep your mouth shut or should I tape that too?" he asked.

"What's going on? Where's Raven?"

"He's out of it. He told you it would get ugly and now it's going to. We're taking over."

Biff tried to force a smile but his cheek was too sore. "Hey guys, this is going a little too far."

"You shouldn't have pissed off Omar. He doesn't like assholes."

"Where is he, I'll apologize."

"You'll have plenty of time for that when he takes you to Ft. Lauderdale."

"Ft. Lauderdale? Why we going there?"

"We're taking a little boat ride." Manny replied.

"You don't expect me to believe this shit. You're just trying to scare me off."

"Have a nice trip." Manny said. "See you on the boat." and he slammed the rear door.

Omar jumped into the front and fired up the Fairlane as he waited for Manny to lead the way in one of the Escalades. Biff immediately started to open conversation, but Omar wouldn't utter a word.

It took fifty minutes to reach Ft. Lauderdale. Manny turned into the road that led to pier 66 while Omar continued on three miles to a small pier, Sunshine Harbor, which housed only six boats.

Manny paid for the Boston Whaler with cash and motored out of pier 66 at four-fifty. The sun was starting to set, so he lit up his running lights as he headed south for Sunshine Harbor. By the time he docked the boat and tied it to the pier it was five-thirty and the last light of the day was all but gone. He made a quick check of the other boats moored in the pier. Except for one boat which showed a dim light escaping from its cabin, the place was deserted. Manny blinked his flashlight three times toward the parking lot. The car blinked its lights back at him.

Omar cut the tape around Biff's ankles and ordered him out of the car. Biff was sweating profusely and asked Omar to wipe his face, but he didn't respond and remained silent. He took out Biff's Beretta and shoved him toward the boat with it. After Biff was secured in a seat Omar taped his ankles again and headed back to the car. He returned with the two fifty pound weights and the chain.

Manny had the engine running and the boat untied and when Omar returned he made a wide turn and headed east for open water. Biff started to talk. "Okay guys I'm scared, Okay? Let's go back and we'll talk this over." Omar slapped a piece of tape over Biff's mouth.

Manny kept the boat headed east until they were five miles off shore. As he slowed and turned the engine to idle, Omar began stringing the chain through the weights. Biff was thrashing violently and was trying to speak. Both men ignored him as Omar swung the chain around Biff's waist and cinched it tight. Finally Manny ripped the tape off

Biff's mouth.

Tears were streaming down Biff's face. "Please, please don't do this," he pleaded. "Call Raven."

"You don't get it do you?" Manny said. "The doc actually wanted to give you a pass, but we're not about to lose a chance at a million dollars."

"I won't get in your way, honest. I'll go home tonight. Please, please call Raven."

Manny and Omar sat in silence; the only sound was the chattering of Biff's teeth. Finally Manny picked up his cell and made the call. "He wants a pass. What should we do; I don't trust him?" Manny listened, nodded his head, and said "Okay we'll do it."

"No, you can't," Biff screamed.

"Take it easy," Manny replied. "Brett said to put you on a plane home."

Biff cried all the way back to the pier and during the car trip to Miami. Omar released the cuffs and ordered Biff into the airport. They headed straight to the men's room. "Clean yourself up you lucky bastard," Omar said. "You don't know how close you came."

Omar checked the departure board and spotted a Red Eye direct to San Francisco. He asked Biff for his wallet and took out three hundred and twenty dollars for the ticket. At eleven thirty-five he called Brett. "I just kissed our friend goodbye."

"Nice job, Omar. Manny's already back. See you at breakfast."

CHAPTER 39

Rob arrived at the airport at ten o'clock on Friday morning, two hours before his passengers were scheduled to show up; flying to the Bahamas involved several extra procedures he had to attend to. The first was an international flight plan that he wanted in the system an hour before departure. The distance between West Palm and Nassau was less than two hundred miles and the weather was clear so he filed a visual instead of an instrument flight plan.

Next, he rented a Coast Guard approved life vest for everyone on board, a requirement for all private aircraft travelling to the Bahamas. He picked up a manifest form which needed to be filled out and turned over to the customs agents in Nassau, but he purposely waited to list the names of the passengers. They would have to display passports and he knew Antonio would be talking to him sometime before departure.

The last order of business was a pre-flight inspection of the Citation and the loading of fuel. Rob had an extra passenger on this trip. In addition to the three couples and himself, he had to make room for the bodyguard, Omar. There was seating for an eighth person in the back of the craft on the seat that doubled as a potty. Omar would have no choice; the potty would be his.

The Citation would use about a hundred gallons in each direction so Rob only filled the tanks with two hundred. He could keep the weight down and then refuel in Nassau before his return.

Antonio and Maria arrived at eleven-thirty, a half hour before departure. Antonio set their suitcase down in the lobby and spotted a pilot well dressed in black slacks, a white shirt with epaulets, and black tie, inspecting the Citation. He approached him. "Are you Rob?" he asked.

Rob, who had some grease on his fingers, wiped his hands on a towel and extended his right hand, "Yes, you must be Antonio. I hear you're my co-pilot," he answered.

Antonio took his hand. "Nice to meet you captain. Could we have a word in private?"

"Sure, let's go into the plane."

Rob took a seat in the passenger cabin and

Antonio sat down opposite him. "I've got a little problem," Antonio said.

"Can I help?" Rob asked.

"I hope so, here's my situation. I got into a little trouble out west a while back. I had to change my name, but I never got a new passport. I know we have to show passports and you have to list them on the manifest. Are you okay with using my former name and passport?"

Rob smiled. "Antonio, you must know who my boss is. I have to do this all the time for his clients. It's not a problem."

"That's great," Antonio sighed. "Just one more thing. I'd appreciate if you kept this just between the two of us. I'd prefer Carlos and Manny didn't know about it."

"I'm good with it. Let's see the passport for the manifest." Antonio handed it to Rob and he copied the name onto the form: John Thomas Talbot.

At noon sharp a Lincoln Town Car and a Cadillac Escalade arrived with the five other passengers. Rob loaded the luggage in the plane and helped the passengers to their seats. Carlos and Marcella took side by side seats. Manny told Carmen and Maria to take the opposing ones, while he took the seat behind the cockpit. Omar kept his head bent away from the ceiling as he made his way to the rear potty seat. Rob directed Antonio to the right co-pilot seat as he latched the door shut and then he settled into the left pilot seat.

Rob and Antonio put on the headsets, and Rob

handed the check list to Antonio. "Why don't you help me through this."

"Glad to," Antonio said, as he prepared to read it out loud to Rob.

"How long since you've flown?" Rob asked.

"About six months, but never anything like this. I flew a Baron 58."

"They all fly the same. Pull to go up, push to go down."

Antonio laughed. "I know better than that. This is a complex machine."

"Once we get to altitude, I'll let you take the controls and you can get a feel for it."

"That would be great," Antonio responded.

The takeoff was uneventful and once in the climb, Rob dialed 122.4 on his number two radio and opened his flight plan to Nassau. He leveled off at thirteen thousand five hundred feet and turned toward Antonio. "Your airplane," he said.

"You sure?"

"Give it a try; it's just straight and level flight."

Antonio took the wheel with delight and essentially steered while the plane propelled toward the Bahamas at just under three hundred miles an hour. When Rob calculated they were ten minutes out, he took control of the plane and started a descent. As soon as the island came into view, he dialed up Nassau radio on 124.2 and closed his flight plan.

As usual, Rob greased the jet onto the runway. "Nice landing," Antonio said.

Rob laughed. "We both know only passengers judge the flight by the landing."

Antonio smiled back. "That's so true. You can take them through rain, ice and turbulence without a comment, but if you bump the landing they say it was a horrible flight."

A stretch limousine approached the Citation after Rob had shut down the engines. A customs officer came out of the office and observed the process as the driver transferred the luggage from the plane into the trunk of the car. Meanwhile the passengers followed Rob into the office where a dark skinned officer was inspecting the manifest and the passports.

Antonio separated from the line. "I forgot my carry case in the cockpit. I'll catch up," he said, as he headed back to the plane. By the time he returned, the others were already loading into the limo. He handed his passport to the officer, got it stamped, jogged to the waiting car and jumped in. "Sorry," he said, as he smiled at Rob.

"Where are we headed?" Maria asked.

"We're going to that new hotel on Paradise Island, Trump Plaza," Marcella answered.

"It's really cool," Carmen added.

After check in they were led to the top floor of the Beach Towers overlooking the blue-green waters of the Caribbean. Carlos and Marcella were shown to a two bedroom suite while the other two couples, and Rob, and Omar were led to plush single rooms. "Let's all meet in our suite for cocktails around seven. I made reservations at eight in the dining room," Carlos said as the couples headed toward their rooms.

Maria and Antonio arrived at the suite right on time at seven o'clock and were met by Omar who was discreetly guarding the door by walking up and down the hallway. He nodded to them and opened the door to the living room with a keycard. Marcella and Carmen greeted them as they entered, while the men, dressed in their blue suits, were in a corner talking. A bartender approached to take drink orders, after which the ladies began complimenting each other on their choice of cocktail dresses, and Antonio drifted toward the men's corner. As he approached, he heard Carlos say to Manny in a loud voice, "Can you raise the last ten and half million, or not?"

Before Manny could answer, Carlos spotted Antonio and dropped the conversation as he raised a finger toward his mouth. "Hello, Antonio, how are the accommodations?"

"Fabulous, I've never heard of this hotel. How new is it?"

"Built in 1998, so about two years," Carlos replied.

The bartender arrived with the drinks and a plate of hot hors d'oeuvres. "To a great weekend," Carlos said raising his glass. The other two men acknowledged the toast and from across the room the ladies raised their glasses.

"I apologize; did I interrupt a business

conversation?" Antonio asked.

"No, not at all. We were just talking about financing for a new project," Manny said. "It can wait. Let's join the ladies."

Carlos had arranged for the best table in the open air section of the restaurant overlooking the water and small boat harbor. He took the patriarch seat at the head with Marcella at his side. The other two couples filled in the other four chairs, while Omar sat by himself at a small table in the corner on the patio. Rob purposely was not part of this group and took his dinner in his room.

By ten o'clock everyone was stuffed and Carlos pushed his chair away from the table. "Anyone up for some gambling?"

"Sure," Manny answered.

Carlos handed each of his guests a thousand dollar chip and said, "Good luck everyone, we'll catch up tomorrow. Marcella and I are headed for bed."

CHAPTER 40

While Antonio and Maria were being entertained in the Bahamas, Brett and Annie were breathing a sigh of relief. At least for this weekend they could expose themselves in town without the fear of running into J.T. and blowing the whole operation. "How about a dinner out tonight?" Brett asked.

"That sounds great. Any place in mind?"

"I read about a beautiful spot on the top floor of The Breakers Resort Hotel. It has a fabulous view. I'll give 'em a call."

The weather was unusually warm for January. Normally seventy-five was the average, but the entire week it had been over eighty. Annie wore a light cotton dress with high heeled sandals and Brett wore a pair of silk slacks with a cotton shirt.

"It is beautiful here, isn't it?" Annie said.

"Yes it is, but I can't wait to get back to our humble abode in California."

"We are splurging a little with this lifestyle. Speaking of California, Samantha got our embryos last Monday. It all seems surreal."

Brett didn't answer; he just sat and reflected. Finally, he said, "Annie, I'm really happy. The next twenty years are going to be the best of our lives. Even if this whole Florida deal implodes, it won't change our future."

"I agree," she said, as she placed her hand on his where the cast used to be. "By the way, I've been waiting for a special time to tell you this; my lawyer called with good news, the annulment went through. I'm officially a single woman named Annie Frazier."

Brett opened up into a wide grin. "Wasn't that the name of the girl I fell in love with in college twenty-five years ago?"

"I'm trying to remember," Annie replied. "Yeah, I believe that was her name."

After dinner as they were waiting for their car to be brought around, Brett said, "I can't believe it's still almost eighty outside. How about a swim in the ocean when we get home?"

"Even with this warm air it's a little cold in the water, isn't it?"

"Let's find out."

Annie put on a blue bikini. Even though she was in her early forties, she had never given birth and her figure was as firm as when she was twenty-five. "Wow, do you look sexy," Brett said.

"Like you've never seen me naked," she responded.

"Naked is nice, but it's much sexier when there's just a little bit left to the imagination. You really do look great."

Brett pulled on a floral print suit, grabbed two towels and a blanket and took Annie's hand as they headed to the beach. The moon was full and reflected off the water like a spotlight from the sky.

"You first," Annie said.

Brett was beginning to wonder if this was such a good idea after all. It felt a little colder than he thought it would when he put his toes in. "Hey, maybe we should go to the pool."

"No way, this was your idea, get in there."

Brett took the towel off his shoulders and sprinted into the surf. "Come on in, it's great."

Annie dropped her towel and made a bee line toward Brett. "You liar, it's only about seventy. I'm freezing," she said through shattering teeth.

"I know, but if I told you the truth, I'd be alone in here."

They both laughed and headed back to the sand with goose bumps popping out all over their skin. "Take this towel," Brett said, as he spread out the oversized blanket on the beach.

Annie took it and then lay down on the blanket

where Brett cuddled in next to her. He folded the big blanket over the top of them and they huddled together shivering, allowing their own body heat to slowly warm them up. Brett pulled Annie closer and kissed her on the side of her neck. "You taste salty," he whispered.

"I thought you always said I tasted sweet."

"Sweet and salt go great together," he said, as he opened his mouth and kissed her on the lips.

They held each other tightly as the chill from the water disappeared and the heat from their bodies warmed them under the blanket. Brett ran his hand under the tiny string that held Annie's bikini top and fiddled with the knot until he finally untied it. He let it drop onto the blanket and then ran his hand over her left breast. The cold water had caused her nipples to stand erect and he took one between his thumb and forefinger. "You're still cold." He said.

"Yeah, but I'm getting warmer real fast."

Brett kissed her again and ran his hand under the tiny cloth covering Annie's left buttock. He caressed the firm muscle and then slowly ran his finger toward the front of her suit. He could feel her excitement flow onto his fingers. "Slip it off," he said.

Annie reached down and wriggled out of the bathing suit bottom. Brett spread her legs and tickled the inside of her thighs as he moved his head down and kissed her nipples. "Aren't you going to take off your suit?" She asked.

"Later," he said, as he dropped his head under the blanket and worked his tongue down her body until it was under her navel. He spread her legs further apart and soon he was between them as Annie lifted her knees toward her chest and thrust her head back on the blanket.

It didn't take long for Annie to climax and grab the back of Brett's suit with both hands. He lifted his hips up to assist in the operation and Annie did the rest as she moved her hands over his erection. "I thought cold water causes shrinkage." She said. "Maybe physics has been defied."

He laughed as he eased inside her. They didn't move; just stayed locked together and kissed softly. "Aren't you going to move?" She finally asked.

"I really don't want to. I love the way this feels."

After ten minutes, he withdrew and as they rolled over on their sides Annie started to speak. "Why didn't you…"

Brett put his index finger over her lips. "I love you, Annie. I don't need that to prove it."

She kissed him back. "I love you too," she said, and pulled him close again.

CHAPTER 41

January is the driest month of the year in the Bahamas, and Saturday was a carbon copy of the previous day. The sun was shining, the temperature was eighty degrees and the ocean shimmered with the same gorgeous blue-green color. Carlos and Marcella decided to have a late breakfast in the terrace dining room and as they walked through the marble tiled entry, Marcella spotted Antonio and Maria and gave a tug on Carlos's sleeve. Carlos picked up on it immediately and they headed toward their table.

"Mind if we join you?" Carlos asked.

Antonio looked up and seeing Carlos jumped to his feet. "Please, please. Didn't see you come in," he said, while pulling out a chair for Marcella.

"How was the gambling?" Carlos asked.

"It was really fun. Maria won five hundred and I broke even. By the way that was very generous of you to finance the evening. As a matter of fact, it's very generous of you to include us in this weekend."

"It's my pleasure," Carlos replied. "I'm very lucky. I make a lot of money and I like sharing it with our friends."

"Well, thanks for including us as friends," Antonio said.

After breakfast Marcella invited Maria to take a tour of the resort jewelry shop, leaving the two men together at the table. When the women were out of sight, Carlos turned to Antonio.

"I think you said you have a background in finance didn't you?"

"Yes, well I was a financial planner. I worked with personal clients on short and long term goals and also sold a few products like insurance."

"Any chance you could drop by my office at the estate next week. Manny is having a little difficulty with the financing of a new deal for me, and I'd like to get your input."

"Certainly," Antonio replied. "I'm flattered, but I think you may be playing in a bigger league than I."

"You never know when you'll get called up to the majors. How about Wednesday around noon? We'll have lunch."

"I'll be there."

Saturday evening Carlos took the group to the dinner show in the cabaret and by midnight everyone was back in their rooms packing for the trip home Sunday morning.

Rob took a cab to the airport at eight-thirty, an hour and half before departure. While performing his pre-flight inspection, he had the fuel truck replenish the hundred gallons he had used on the trip over. That was the easy part; the hardest task was preparing all the paperwork and complying with the regulations for leaving the Bahamas and re-entering the United States.

Once again he filed an international visual flight plan from Nassau to West Palm Beach, after which he placed a call to U.S. Customs with his estimated time of arrival. After the call he prepared a U.S. Arrival Report and a Customs Declaration Form for each person or family on board. To save time during boarding, he went to the customs office and paid the Bahamas departure tax of twenty dollars for himself and also for each of his seven passengers. The rest would be easy; fill out a Bahamas Customs General Declaration Form and turn back everyone's immigration cards.

The trip back only took forty-five minutes; however, everyone on the plane had to clear U.S. Customs in West Palm Beach with their luggage in tow. Rob was watching closely as Antonio went through the line with his J.T. Talbot passport; he had no problem, the agents were more intent on questioning the slick looking Enrique and his tough looking bodyguard.

It took another forty minutes before all the luggage was loaded into their cars and they were exiting the parking lot. Omar was driving the Lincoln Town Car with Carlos and Marcella in the back seat. As they passed Antonio, Carlos dropped his window. "Wednesday," he called out.

Antonio waved. "Noon," he replied.

CHAPTER 42

Brett and Annie were lounging next to the pool when the cars circled into the drive. Before they had time to dry off, Carmen came running out on the deck, threw her arms around his neck, and gave Brett a big kiss on the cheek. "Oh, Brett, I love it down here. That was the best weekend I've ever had; food, booze, gambling, shows and sun. Thank you."

Brett pried himself loose. "You're welcome. Did you get any work done?"

"All I did was dress up and look pretty. I think Enrique and Manny did the heavy lifting."

By now the rest of the group had joined them on the deck, and Annie began pouring ice tea for everyone. Brett looked over at Enrique. "Wednesday,"

Enrique said. "It's time."

Brett, Annie, Carmen, and Manny left the estate by eleven a.m. on Wednesday morning; not taking any chance that Antonio might show up early. At eleven forty-five Antonio drove up to the gate and was greeted by Omar. He acknowledged Antonio, punched in the digits to open the gate, and waved him through. Marcella met him at the front door and directed him to Carlos' office.

Enrique had put a few personal touches on Carlos' office décor. He bought a map of Colombia, placed a felt pen circle around the city of Bucaramanga, had it framed in bamboo, and hung it behind his desk chair. He also brought their wedding portrait, taken of Marcella and him in an old church in Mexico thirty years ago, which he placed on his desk.

Antonio knocked gently on the open office door. Carlos glanced up from his desk and motioned him in. "Antonio, right on time. Come in, sit down and make yourself comfortable."

"Beautiful office, I love the old photo of you and Marcella."

Carlos walked around to the front of the desk, picked up the picture, and looked at it nostalgically. "Taken in 1970 back in Colombia. Beautiful wasn't she?"

"She still is," Antonio replied.

Carlos pointed to the map on the wall. "That

church in the picture is over a thousand years old. It's still standing right there in our home town of Bucaramanga."

"Do you go back often?"

"Only for business. The drug wars have pretty much wiped out our families."

"I'm sorry," Antonio said.

"That's the life I chose," Carlos said. "It's bittersweet." He took one more lingering glance at the photo and set it back on his desk. "Let's go out on the terrace. Marcella's fixed a little lunch."

Marcella brought a basket covered by a napkin with steam rising from it. "Have you ever eaten any Colombian food?" she asked Antonio.

"I can't say that I have."

"This is called Pandebono," she said as she removed the napkin. "Try it."

Antonio separated a piece of the bread and took a bite. "My God, that's delicious. What's it made of?"

Marcella smiled, "It's actually corn flour mixed with cheese and eggs. We used to eat it with a soup called Puchero, but today I'm afraid you'll have to make do with chicken salad."

Antonio smiled, "That will be fine."

After Marcella had served the salad and the Pandebono, she quietly slipped back into the main house, leaving the men to themselves.

Carlos took two beers out of the ice bucket and poured a glass for each of them. "Antonio, I'm guessing you're in your early fifties?"

"Fifty-two, actually."

"I'm impressed you did well enough to retire at such a young age. What are you going to do to keep yourself busy?"

"I haven't given it much thought really."

"Ever considered getting back into finance?"

"I'm not sure what you mean exactly."

"Well, Manny has been setting up the financing for all my deals. It's a big job, and right now he's about ten million short for my new project. Maybe you could give him some ideas."

"That's flattering, but I wouldn't dream of giving advice to Manny. He's a very capable guy."

Carlos poured himself another glass of beer and held the bottle up toward Antonio. "Just a half glass," Antonio said.

"I understand what you're saying, and I, too, believe Manny is very capable, but for the first time he just seems stuck on this deal. If I set up a time, would you meet with him and kick some ideas around?"

"I don't know what advice I could give, but I certainly would meet with him. Just a little afraid he might be insulted though."

Carlos flashed a wide smile, exposing a corner of gold on his upper right canine. "I don't think you have to worry about that. He's the one who suggested it."

CHAPTER 43

It was Monday January 30th, almost a month since they had arrived in Palm Beach. Annie was nervous as a cat and kept looking at her watch every five minutes as she paced the bedroom floor. Finally Brett said, "Call the doctor already. Let's find out."

Annie looked at her watch again. "It's only a little after nine on the West Coast. I doubt they know yet."

"Just call, the worst they can say is 'call back later.'"

"You sure?"

"Call."

Annie scrolled through the favorite numbers

on her phone, hitting quick dial, when she found Dr. Rappaport. "San Francisco Fertility Clinic," a voice said after the second ring.

"Good morning, this is Annie Frazier; I'm inquiring about the results of a pregnancy test."

"Just a moment please," the receptionist said as she shuffled through a stack of papers. "Could it be under any other name?"

"Try Raven," she responded. "By the way the test was done on a surrogate, Samantha O'Brian."

"Oh yes, it just came in. Let me have Dr. Rappaport talk to you," she said as she put Annie on hold.

Sweat broke out on Annie's forehead. "You okay?" Brett asked

"Just nervous, I'm on hold."

Suddenly a deep voice boomed through the phone speaker. "Annie, I was just going to call. No beating around the bush, she's pregnant."

Annie couldn't hold back as tears rolled down her cheeks. She tried to speak, but no sounds came out. "Did you hear me all right?" the doctor asked.

This time she squeezed out words. "Thank you. Thank you so much."

Brett eased the phone away from Annie. "Hello, Doc, it's Brett. From Annie's response I'm guessing things are going good and we're pregnant."

"Yes, Brett, we're going to watch Samantha closely and do a sonogram in four weeks, around the end of February."

"That's great. Does Samantha know yet?"

"You want to give her the news?"

"Yes, we'll call her right now. Thanks again."

Brett put his arms around Annie and held her tight. He couldn't hold back the tears either and they both just held on and let them flow.

Annie dialed Samantha's number and as soon as she answered, Annie said, "You're pregnant."

"Annie, are you sure?"

"We just talked to the doctor. How are you feeling?"

"I'm wonderful. When will I see you guys?"

"We'll be home in about two weeks. Let's go to dinner and celebrate."

"I'll look forward to it."

"Take good care of yourself now."

"Don't worry, I will."

Annie put the phone down on the end table and gave Brett a kiss. "Will you marry me?" she asked.

He looked surprised. "Are you sure?"

"I'm positive."

"Then you know the answer; it's yes!"

By the time they arrived on the terrace it was almost one and everyone else was finished eating. "Wondering if you guys were skipping lunch." Manny said.

"We got side tracked," Annie responded. "But we have some good news."

Both Marcella and Carmen sensed what was coming and they embraced Annie. "Is she?" Marcella asked.

"Yes, we're pregnant."

The entire group started to whoop and holler. Omar, with muscles bulging, picked Annie up and swung her hundred and twenty pounds over his head. Everyone else was clapping their hands together and laughing.

"We have more good news," Annie said, as Omar set her back on her feet.

"What could top this?" Enrique asked.

"There's going to be a wedding here at the estate."

Carmen couldn't contain herself. She was jumping up and down. "I love weddings, they're so romantic. When is it?"

Brett looked at Annie. Annie looked at Brett. "How 'bout this Saturday?" Brett said.

Annie picked up a glass and held it upside down near her mouth and talked into it like a microphone. "Saturday, February 4th, 2001. You are all invited to the wedding of Annie Frazier and Brett Raven on the beach at the home of Carlos Antonio and Marcella Rojas. Please rsvp within the next three minutes."

Brett located a retired judge and arranged for him to be at the estate by three p.m. Annie called the same caterers who had done the dinner party and scheduled them to be at the house by two-thirty with a full seafood menu. Omar and Rob rented a large tent canopy under which they placed a small table for the judge to use, along with six dining room chairs for the guests. Marcella and Carmen dissected the estates' flower gardens and created a gorgeous arrangement of Orange and Lemon Symphony along with a touch of Flambe, which they set on the table top. They also put together a lovely hand bouquet for Annie which was made up entirely of fragrant Pink Innocence.

All the guests were clad in shorts; however, the bride and groom went semi-formal for the occasion. Brett put on his blue linen jacket over a white silk tee shirt and tan shorts and Annie wore a white sun dress, white sandals and a floppy white hat.

Brett stood under the tent with the judge as Enrique walked Annie from the house to the beach. She looked radiant, dressed in all white holding her pink bouquet. Brett took Annie's arm from him and then Enrique found the remaining dining room chair.

What a difference twenty years of twists and turns had made, Brett and Annie both thought to themselves. In 1980 they were married in a church with two hundred of their parent's friends looking on. Today they were being married on a beach and it was being witnessed by a different, but closer set of friends: two gangsters, a wife and girlfriend, a thirty-two year old multi-millionaire, and a three hundred pound bodyguard.

After "man and wife," Brett got the first kiss, but he was quickly pushed aside as the guests smothered Annie with affection.

The food was outrageous: pounds of Shelled Lobster, Blue Crabs, and Rock Shrimp. As a special treat there were deep fried Gator Tails and Conch Fritters, and for dessert there was fresh Key Lime Pie adorned with a little bride and groom statute on top. Enrique had insisted on buying the alcohol and no one was surprised when a case of Dom Perignon Champagne showed up.

By nine o'clock, with the food and champagne almost gone, the party began to wind down. Enrique and Manny, along with Marcella and Carmen, asked Brett and Annie if they could have a word.

Once inside the library, Enrique asked Brett, "Is our cut still going to be around four hundred thousand?"

Brett was taken back. He hadn't expected to talk business on this day and wondered what would prompt Enrique to bring it up at such an awkward time. Maybe the group was unhappy with the arrangement. "I certainly hope so, but remember we don't have anything until the deal is done."

"We know that," Enrique said. "But if it goes through, we want to change it up a little."

"How so?" Brett asked, with trepidation.

"We know you're not making any profit on this deal." Manny said. "We also know it's going to cost close to a hundred thou for your new baby."

"We want our cut reduced by a hundred thousand." Enrique said. "That hundred is a wedding present to our good friends for their new baby."

Brett and Annie were dumbfounded; neither

could speak.

Manny detected a little tear forming in the corner of Brett's eye. "Now don't get all mushy on us Doc," he said. "Make us godparents if you like, but that's our present to both of you and your child."

Annie couldn't control herself. She hugged both women so hard they lost their breath.

CHAPTER 44

The intercom buzzed in Manny's office. "Mr. Antonio Russ to see you," the receptionist announced.

"Send him in Francene."

Manny rose to shake Antonio's hand and pulled out a chair facing his desk. "Thanks for coming," Manny said.

"No problem, my time is pretty open these days. I have to admit though; I really don't think I'm qualified to give you any fund raising advice."

Manny reached in a drawer and took out a bulging manila folder, which was stuffed full of papers, and flopped it down on the desktop. "This is Carlos' new deal. He has personally put thirty million into it and I've raised an additional forty. Problem is, the project won't go if I can't raise a total of eighty and a half million. As you can see, I'm ten and a half short and Carlos is chomping at the bit. The money has to be in Colombia in ten days."

"Can't Carlos provide it?"

"No, he's tapped out at thirty. What's more, he'll forfeit ten million if the financing falls short and the deal goes sour. I'm getting worried, Antonio. Carlos is a good friend, but money always comes first. If I don't get the financing, this will be my last project with him."

"I really don't have any ideas for you," Antonio said apologetically.

They sat in silence while Manny appeared to struggle with the problem. Finally he spoke, "Would you consider putting up the ten and half million?"

Antonio was a little embarrassed. Apparently Carlos and Manny thought he was a bigger player than he actually was. "Manny, I'd do it if I could, but I just don't have that kind of money."

Manny looked perplexed. "I know it's none of my business, but you did retire at fifty-two. I was under the impression you socked a lot away."

Antonio regretted bragging about his accomplishments. "I'm comfortable and I'm not opposed to investing, but ten and a half million is just beyond my capability."

They sat in silence again until Antonio finally

broke it. "If it's only for a month or two, I could probably come up with half that amount, but I can't afford to lose it."

Manny sat in deep thought for a few more minutes. "I have an idea," he finally said. "Carlos has always been opposed to having me put any of my personal money into his deals. He doesn't think I should profit at both ends. What if I put up five and a quarter and you put up five and a quarter, but we keep it between ourselves. As far as Carlos would know, you're putting up the entire ten and a half."

"Would that work?" Antonio asked.

"This would have to stay between the two of us. If Carlos found out, he'd can me on the spot."

"I can keep the secret," Antonio said, "but what's my return and what's my security?"

"I think I mentioned to you last time we met, that Carlos is very generous with his investors. He pays a hundred percent and usually only keeps the money for thirty to forty-five days."

"So we'd each double our money in less than two months?"

"So far it's worked every time."

Antonio wanted the deal desperately, but was smart enough to know there was always a risk of losing all his money. "Is there any way you could get me, or should I say us, some security?"

Manny thought for a moment. "Carlos only did it once, when he needed to close a deal quickly, and he put up his estate for security with an investor. I did all the paperwork."

"Do you think he'd consider it again?"

"I could check. If he agreed, it would cover my ass also." Manny put his right index finger to his lips for silence from Antonio as he dialed his cell phone. "Carlos, I may have the ten and a half. Antonio has the cash and is willing to invest." Manny paused listening to the other side of the phone conversation. "Only one problem, this will tap him out and he's afraid of losing it. Would you consider putting up the estate like you did on the Contreras deal?" Manny listened again. "Okay, I'll keep looking, but time is getting short." He hung up.

"Bad news?" Antonio asked.

"Carlos is not one to make hasty decisions. He told me to keep looking for a regular investor, but between you and me, I think he'll go for it. There are no other investors this late in the game."

"If Carlos gives the okay, how do you and I pool our money?"

"The only thing in writing will be between you and Carlos. I'll get you my half of the investment and we'll operate on a handshake."

"Five and a quarter million is a lot for you to trust me with."

"I don't have to trust you, only your judgment. I trust that the last thing you would want is the mob chasing you to get my money back."

Antonio forced a laugh. "You're right, I certainly don't need that. Just making over five million in a month or two is good enough for me."

Manny didn't smile back. "I'm going to run it by Carlos again this afternoon. Can I call you on your cell?"

"Sure, it'll stay glued to me."

Manny stood up signaling the end of the meeting. "Wait for my call; and Antonio remember, this is our secret. When you talk to Carlos, you are the investor and it's your ten and half million. My name never comes up."

"You've burned it into my brain. Don't worry."

After Antonio left the office, Manny called the Equity Elite Title Company in West Palm Beach. "Title Officer please," he asked.

"My name's Sophia, I'm a title officer."

"Hi Sophia, my name is Emanuel Diaz with Creative Lending and Management over on Okeechobee."

"What can I do for you Mr. Diaz?"

"I need a prelim title report on a parcel over on the island. I don't think we'll be setting up an escrow, so I'd like to pay for it on a fee for service basis, if that works for you."

"That's fine. The fee is five hundred and forty. Can you give me the parcel number?"

Manny took out a copy of the notes, from the Palm Beach County recorder's office, that Brett had made long before this adventure had begun.

PARCEL #001-238-6994
Owner: Dehavilland Family Trust
Appraisal 1998: $16,200,000
Mortgage Holder: None

PARCEL #010-877-2400
Owner: Carlos Alberto Rojas
Appraisal 1996: $17,650,000
Mortgage Holder: None

PARCEL #099-131-6740
Owner: Ruth Clement & Otto Clement
Appraisal 1989: $17,400,000
Mortgage Holder: Bank of America, $4,500,000

"Here it is. Zero, one, zero, dash eight, seven, seven, dash two, four, zero, zero."

"You can pick it up the day after tomorrow," Sophia said. "Anything else you need?"

"Yes, do you by any chance have a standard form for a promissory note and deed of trust?"

"Sure, they're free. I'll leave them with the report."

"Thanks Sophia, see ya day after tomorrow."

As soon as he hung up from the title company, Manny thumbed through the yellow pages under the heading of Real Estate Appraisers. He called the first one on the list, A-1 Appraisers.

"I need a rush appraisal of an estate on the island," he said.

The secretary was very taken with self-importance. "That will cost you quite a bit," she said smugly.

"I don't care what it costs. Can you get it done this week?"

"That depends on our schedule."

"Look, lady," he said angrily. "Either you can do it or you can't. If you want the business, answer by saying 'yes,' and tell me when you'll show up. Otherwise say 'no,' and we'll stop wasting each other's time."

"Yes, two o'clock tomorrow. Have a check ready for fourteen hundred dollars."

"See how easy that was," Manny replied, as he gave her the address of the property. "I'll look for your guy tomorrow."

Before he left the office, Manny called Antonio. "What did he decide?" Antonio asked.

"He decided to go with it. Told me to draw up the documents."

"What do I have to do?"

"Just make sure your funds are liquid and, oh yes; get me an account and routing number so I can get my five and a quarter into your account. I'll call you next week before the deal closes."

"Sounds great. Thanks, Manny."

"No problem, partner," he said, and hung up.

CHAPTER 45

Annie glanced down at the papers piled on Brett's desk and couldn't help but notice the report from Drake Caymen that had arrived a couple months ago. It was the one that Annie had used to make appointments for Marcella and Carmen: *The first and third Thursday of each month she has her nails done at Nails by Nadia in Palm Beach. On the second and fourth Thursday she has a pedicure at Pampered Feet also on the island. Once a month, usually the first week, she has her hair done at Sal's Salon in West Palm.*

She tried to fight the urge but she couldn't control it. She knew it was the wrong thing to do, but she was obsessed with the thought of meeting Maria, the woman who J.T. had married while he was still married to her. She picked up the report and put it back down, then picked it up again and dialed the number scribbled in the margin next to Sal's Salon.

"Sal's Hair Salon. How may I help you?"

"Hi, I'm Maria Russ' secretary. She lost the date and time for her appointment this week. Could you look it up?"

"Sure hang on," the receptionist said, as she thumbed through the appointment book. "Here it is, this Friday at two o'clock."

"Thanks, I'll remind her."

Annie waited an hour, put a wad of gum in her mouth and then dialed the number for Sal's again. The same receptionist answered. Annie chewed the gum between her front teeth. "Hi, my name is Nancy Jergen. Any chance I could pop in this Friday afternoon for a quick wash and blow dry?"

"Sure, how about four-thirty?"

"Anything earlier, around two, two-thirty?"

"We can squeeze you in at two-thirty."

"Great, I'll be there."

"See you Friday," the receptionist said, and hung up.

Annie arrived forty minutes early, at one fifty, checked in, and took a seat in the reception area. Five minutes later a tall blonde woman with an attractive figure came through the door and took a seat across from Annie. Annie smiled; the blonde smiled back. "Come here often?" Annie said.

"Every month, Sal is an artist. You?"

"First time. We're from California, just down here on vacation."

Just then the receptionist appeared. "Mrs. Russ, Sal's ready for you."

Maria went into the work area and began talking to a good looking, surprisingly masculine, stylist, who Annie assumed was Sal. She stared at Maria for a full thirty minutes until she was called in for her own wash and dry with Vinny, another handsome, young stylist, wearing a blue apron. She tried to hate the woman, at least dislike her, but the feelings just weren't there. According to Brett, Maria was involved in the fraud; however, she never knew about Annie and never knew about J.T.'s bigamist life style.

Now Annie knew it was a big mistake to have come here. What was she thinking? What did she expect to find out about Maria? She couldn't wait to get away from this place. As soon as her hair was blown dry she tipped Vinny ten dollars, paid the receptionist fifty for the wash and dry, and walked out the front door.

Annie was parked at a meter about a half block to the right. As she exited the salon she glanced to her left and admired a green two door Mercedes that was waiting with its motor running in the white curbed loading zone. For a split second she made eye contact with the driver and she felt as if a fist had punched her in the stomach.

The brain takes a picture and it can replay it over and over again. She only made eye contact for a second, but she knew J.T.'s brain had taken a picture, and it had already been played back to him. She hurried to her car and pulled into traffic on S. Quadrille Blvd, northbound. A glance into her rear view mirror located the green Mercedes about a half block behind. She pushed down the accelerator and headed toward a street sign that read **Flagler Memorial Bridge 1 mile.** While crossing over the bridge to the island she looked again in her mirror, spotting the Mercedes still about three hundred yards behind; she knew she couldn't lead J.T. to the estate. She exited the east side of the bridge and while frantically looking for an escape route, she spied a billboard with a familiar landmark: **The Breakers Palm Beach—Luxury Resort Hotel .7 mi. ahead.** Annie swung her Escalade up to the front of the hotel, jumped out and took a valet parking receipt from the attendant. As she scurried into the lobby she eyed the Mercedes pulling up to the curb about fifty feet behind her.

Annie spotted a sign for the Ladies Room and headed straight for it. Once inside, she locked herself in a stall, took out her cell phone, and with her hand shaking like a leaf, dialed Brett. He answered on the first ring.

"Brett, I can't explain right now, but I'm in the ladies room at The Breakers Hotel. J.T. spotted me and is in a green two door Mercedes out front."

There was silence. "Are you there?'

"Yeah, I'm thinking. Stay where you are. I'll take a cab over and meet you in the coffee shop. I'll call your cell just before I get there."

"Okay, I'm so sorry."

"Just stay where you are. I should be there in a half hour."

It took fifteen minutes for the cab to arrive at the estate and another ten to reach the gates of the hotel. Brett dialed Annie's cell. "I'm here, head for the coffee shop."

Brett paid the driver and casually glanced toward the driveway. The green Mercedes was still parked at the curb behind him.

He spotted Annie at a booth in the back of the dining room and slid in next to her. She was still shaking. "Calm down, calm down, it's going to be all right."

"Brett, this was my fault. I went to the salon where Maria was having her hair done. He must have come to pick her up and was outside in his car when I came out."

"Annie, for God's sake why? Why did you go there?"

"I can't explain, I can't. I felt driven to meet her. It was stupid." She tried to hold back tears, "I've ruined everything for you."

Brett put his arm around her. "It's okay, it's not over. He still has no way to connect us with Carlos and Manny. Let's just play it out. J.T. must think we're staying in this hotel, so we'll just let him keep thinking that."

A waiter appeared to take their order. "Can we get liquor in here?" Brett asked.

"Yes, sir," the waiter responded.

"Two Chevas, no ice."

The Scotch calmed Annie down a bit and she got a hold of herself. "What's next?'

"I'm going to check into the hotel under our own name. I'm sure he'll inquire to see if we're staying here. We can take your car and lose him in traffic, and then we'll head back to the estate."

Brett booked a room for a week and then he and Annie left the lobby and called for the car. The Mercedes was still parked at the curb. Brett got behind the wheel of the Escalade and crossed back over the Flagler Bridge heading west. The Mercedes was following a couple hundred yards behind. In about a mile a sign appeared: **I 95 South – Miami 70 mi.** Brett jumped ahead of an old pickup truck and accelerated into the on ramp. The Mercedes was trapped behind the clunker and before it could get on the Interstate, Brett had already exited at the next off ramp. They drove around West Palm for twenty minutes until they were sure J.T. was not back on their tail, and then they headed to the estate.

Brett called a meeting and everyone assembled within fifteen minutes on the terrace. "We've had a stroke of bad luck. J.T. accidentally spotted Annie in town. I don't know if he'll get spooked and run or if he'll stick around for the money and go through with the deal."

Enrique asked, "Should we fold it up?"

"No way, Antonio has no connection between Annie and me and you guys. Just stay in the game and we'll see what he does."

Just then Manny's cell rang. "It's J.T., let me get it." He put the phone on speaker. "Hey, Antonio, what's up?"

"Listen, Manny, can I meet with you and Carlos? You know I'm in for the money, but I need some help with a situation that just came up."

Manny gave everyone thumbs up. "Sure, when?"

"How about your office in an hour?"

"We'll meet you there."

CHAPTER 46

Manny and Carlos pulled up to the office building at six-thirty p.m. It was locked and J.T. was waiting outside. Manny searched for a key on his ring, opened the front door and then the elevator. Everyone had left for the evening so the trio headed straight to the conference room.

"So Antonio, what's so important that we have to meet at cocktail time?" Carlos asked.

"Okay, I promised Manny I'd come up with the $10.5 million, but I need you guys to do me a favor first."

"Sure, name it," Carlos said.

"I got into some trouble in California a while back. A guy and his wife are tracking me and if they get me, I'm headed for jail and my money is headed south."

"And?" Manny asked.

"I need you to get rid of them for me."

There was silence, then Carlos asked, "Do you mean what I think you mean?"

"I don't care how you get rid of them; I don't even want to know. I just need them off my ass. Come on, you guys must have faced a problem like this before."

Manny looked at Carlos and Carlos gave him an affirmative nod. "How do we find them?" Manny asked.

J.T. pulled out an old picture of himself with Brett and Annie. They were all smiling and standing next to the Baron that J.T. later crashed in Baja. Their arms were on each other's shoulders and Annie wore the heart shaped necklace that Brett had given her for her thirtieth birthday. "Here they are," he said, as he handed the photo to Manny. "They're staying at The Breakers, room 6212."

"When?" Manny asked.

"When is the deal closing?' Antonio responded

"In five days," Carlos said.

"Tomorrow then."

"We'll call you day after tomorrow." Manny said, and they all shook hands and left the office.

Everyone was still milling around the terrace when Enrique and Manny returned. "You won't believe this," Enrique said.

"What?" Brett asked.

"He put a contract out on you guys. We get the money after we dispose of you."

"That son of a bitch," Annie said. "What do we do now?"

Brett thought for a moment and then broke into a smile. "This is better than I thought; the deal can still go through."

Everyone looked at Brett in astonishment. "How?" they uttered.

Brett took out his cell and pushed speed dial for #21. The phone rang four times. "Caymen here."

"Hey Drake, it's Brett Raven."

"Doc, what's up?"

"Can you dig up a makeup artist and a photographer by noon tomorrow?"

"No problem, all it takes is money."

"I won't even ask the price, just tell us where and what time."

"I'll call you by nine tomorrow morning. It'll be here in Miami."

"I'll wait for your call," Brett said, and hung up.

Drake called Brett at eight forty-five the next morning. "Here's the address of the studio. Can you be here by eleven?"

"We'll be there."

Brett and Annie gulped down their coffee along with a piece of toast. Brett shook hands with the guys and Annie kissed Marcella and Carmen. "Good Luck," Omar bellowed.

"Yes, good luck," everyone echoed.

The seventy mile trip took an hour and fifteen minutes. Brett got lost in Miami, but still managed to pull up in front of the studio at five to eleven where Drake was waiting out front. "Okay, mystery man. Come in and let us know what's going down."

The makeup artist was a fifty year old woman named Nora, who obviously practiced her art on herself. She had fake eyebrows, fake lashes, capped teeth, and dyed red hair. The photographer, Christophe, looked as if he had just rolled out of bed. He was unshaven, his long hair uncombed, and his deodorant stick was apparently empty. The studio was surprisingly well equipped with props, make up, and camera equipment.

"I want you to murder us in photos," Brett said.

"Say again," Christophe said.

"We need Nora to make us look like we've been murdered and we need you to shoot photos that'll make it look believable."

Nora went to work on Annie first. She used a doughy substance to puff out her cheeks and then added black and blue coloring around her eyes and cheekbones. She placed an oily substance in Annie's hair which stuck it to her forehead and ears. Then she had her put on a disheveled blouse and ripped it from her right shoulder. The final piece of creativity was the appearance of a purple bullet hole above Annie's left eyebrow, where she placed a moist red substance that dripped down her cheek and dried to a semi-solid state. "Christophe, I need a prop for her to lie on; something that looks like a cement floor."

Christophe quickly came up with piece of cardboard that simulated cement. Nora placed an amorphous red rubber pad that looked like dried blood under Annie's head. "Okay, Annie, lie down on this, close your eyes and play dead."

As Annie began to assume the position, Brett spoke up. "Almost forgot. Put this heart shaped necklace on her. It'll seal the deal."

Christophe adjusted lights to a dim mode and started shooting photos. After each set of two, he re-arranged Annie's position and pose. For the last two, he dripped a greasy substance over her head and shoulders giving the appearance of dried sweat. "Okay, Annie, let's get Brett ready."

Nora decided to treat Brett a little differently. She used the same black and blue makeup on his face, but then she had him strip off his shirt. She created the purple bullet hole with the blood just below his left nipple and let it drip down under his belt. Then she had him lie face up on the cardboard and she placed the red rubber pad under the left side of his back.

Christophe said to Brett, "Try eyes open with a blank stare." When he felt Brett had the pose right, he began shooting photos while again changing pose positions after every two shots. He finished up the same way as he had with Annie, by creating a sweaty look. "You guys clean up and go out for lunch. I'll have these developed and dried in a little over an hour."

At lunch Brett and Annie found out Nora had worked in Hollywood for MGM before she fell in love with a starving author and had moved to Florida. She had stories that kept them howling all through their meal; they really liked this woman. When they returned to Christophe's studio, the photos were ready and they were uncanny. It gave Brett and Annie the chills to see themselves as dead bodies; they looked so real, Annie began to tremble. The five of them spent two hours choosing two photos of Annie and two of Brett which they unanimously agreed would appear the most authentic.

"What do we owe you?" Brett asked Drake.

"I'll figure it out with Nora and Christophe. You get going. I'll bill you."

They both shook hands with Drake and Christophe and gave Nora a big hug. "Thanks guys, you were great," Annie said, as they headed for their car with the four photos safely in hand.

CHAPTER 47

Antonio answered on the first ring. "Meet me at my office in half an hour," Manny said.

"Make it forty-five," Antonio said, and hung up.

It was Sunday and there was no one around so Manny left the door open to the reception room. He was at his desk when he heard a light tap on his office door. "Antonio, come in."

Antonio took a chair and said, "Sounds like you have some news for me".

Manny opened an envelope and threw the four photos in front of Antonio. As he picked them up and looked at them, Manny could see the blood drain from his face as it turned ashen gray. There was a wastebasket sitting next to the desk and Antonio grabbed it with both hands and vomited into it.

Manny handed him a Kleenex. "You've got puke all over your left cheek."

Antonio wiped his face and said, "I didn't think you were…"

Manny interrupted him and said angrily, "Don't give me that shit. You knew exactly what you were asking for and what was going to go down."

"But…"

"It's over Antonio, live with it. Those pictures are yours, but I suggest you destroy 'em."

"I, I don't want them."

Manny snatched them back, flipped on the shredder, and fed them into the crunching blades. He opened his top drawer and took out a bottle of Wild Turkey and a paper cup and handed the drink to Antonio. "This is the big leagues, man. If you want to play in them, you better pull yourself together."

"Thanks, I'm okay," he said, as he swallowed the entire offering in one gulp.

"We ready to talk about the deal now?"

"Yeah, I'm ready," he said, his hand still visibly shaking.

"Okay, on Monday I'm putting five and a quarter million into your account. Do you have the numbers I asked for?"

Antonio opened his wallet and handed Manny a piece of paper. "Here they are. It's my investment account at Merrill Lynch."

Manny took the paper, checked for a routing number and account number, and put it under his blotter. "Make sure you give a 'heads up' to your advisor over there. He's going to have to make a wire transfer to get the ten and a half mill moving."

"How does that work? Antonio asked, with a little worry in his voice. "He doesn't send it to Colombia, does he?"

"No way," Manny answered. "Don't worry I've done this dozens of times. I'll lead you through it on Wednesday."

"Is Carlos still okay with putting up the estate for collateral?"

"With all the money he's going to make on this transaction, he's fine with it. I'll have him sign all the documents beforehand, and I'll have them here for you to sign on Wednesday. After the doc's are signed, you'll have your Merrill Lynch guy transfer the funds, and when I get confirmation, I'll go down to the County Recorder's Office and get everything on record to make sure our butts are covered."

"Sounds good. What time Wednesday?"

"Early, about eight o'clock. It takes several hours to get confirmation for a wire transfer of that size."

Antonio got up to leave. "I'll see you at eight on Wednesday. Sorry about earlier."

Manny rose to his feet and took Antonio's hand. "It's all right; I understand this kind of stuff is new to you. Call me when you get my wire transfer on Monday."

CHAPTER 48

Back in August Annie had received $5 million and Brett had received $190 thousand as insurance benefits from the airplane crash in Baja, Mexico. None of the money was ever touched by them; however, it had accrued interest for almost six months.

At nine a.m. on Monday morning Brett called the Miami Bank & Trust where he and Annie had wired the insurance proceeds from California. "Peter Rankin," Brett said, after he was greeted by the receptionist.

A voice came on the line. "Rankin."

Hello, Peter, Brett Raven here. I opened an account for our loan company a couple months ago."

"Brett, I remember very well. Not every day we get a deposit of over $5 million. What can I do for you today?"

"Well, we're placing a big loan. Could you check on our current balance?"

"That was for Creative Lending and Management, I recall. Hang on while I go to the computer." It took about three minutes. "The current balance is five million, three hundred, ninety-eight thousand, and change."

"Perfect. I'd like you to wire five million, two hundred and fifty thousand, to a Merrill Lynch account in West Palm. Will it be there this afternoon?"

"Sure, that's no problem. Give me the routing and account numbers."

Brett read the numbers that Antonio had scribbled on the paper he had given to Manny on Saturday.

"It'll be on its way in an hour."

"Thanks, Peter."

"My pleasure, call me anytime."

At four o'clock Manny called Antonio. "Hey Antonio, I wired the money into your account. Did you get it?"

"I was just going to call you. It arrived from your company and posted about a half hour ago."

"Great, take good care of it till Wednesday."

"Don't worry, I will."

CHAPTER 49

It was Wednesday February 15th; six weeks since the group had arrived at the estate in Palm Beach. Everyone was in a somber mood at seven a.m. It was their last breakfast together.

"Hey, guys," Brett said. "What's with the long faces? Today is payday."

Carmen looked at him with damp eyes. "I was hoping it would never end. I love this place, and I love all you guys, and now it's over."

Brett went to her and gave her a hug. "The Florida experience is over, but our friendship isn't."

"Will we still see you guys when we're back in California?" Carmen whispered softly.

Annie came over to help console her. "Carmen,

Brett and I consider everyone in this room our truest friends. True friends stay true friends and it doesn't matter if they're in Florida or California, or anywhere else."

Enrique, never missing a chance for a toast, raised his orange juice glass in the air. "To friendship," he said.

"To friendship," everyone repeated, with smiles finally appearing on their faces as they downed their juice.

"Thanks, everyone," Brett said. "Thanks for a fabulous job and thanks for the friendship."

"Hey it's seven-thirty. I have to meet Antonio at eight," Manny said, as he stuffed a piece of toast in his mouth and headed for the door. "What time at the airport?"

Brett turned to Rob. "Will two o'clock work?"

"I'll have the plane ready."

Antonio was waiting in the reception room when Manny arrived. "You look ready for action," Manny said.

"Didn't want to be late."

"Let's go into the conference room," Manny responded, as he led the way. "Coffee?"

"No, I'm fine."

Manny opened his briefcase and laid out a row of documents on the long table. "Okay, let's go through these. I know you've done these financial transactions before, but I'll still explain each one, and I'll have you sign where needed."

"Sounds good," Antonio said.

"The first one is the appraisal on the property. You can look through the detail later, but the main item is the value placed on the property by the appraiser. You can see he valued it at nineteen million four hundred thousand."

Antonio glanced through the fifteen page document which described the property both in words and photos. "That's pretty good collateral for a ten and a half million loan," he said, as he placed it back on the table.

Manny moved it to the end of the table. "That's your copy. We'll keep your stuff separated." He picked up the next set of papers. "This is a preliminary title report. You can look through it, but the main thing here is to note that Carlos Alberto Rojas is the owner of the property and there are no loans or liens against it."

Antonio gave it a once over and placed it in his pile on top of the appraisal. "Looks good," he said.

Manny next went to a document which had been drawn up in triplicate. "This is the promissory note for ten and a half million dollars. It states that Carlos promises to pay you back the principal plus an additional ten and half million in interest. The term is ninety days."

"Didn't you say we would get our money back sooner?"

"Most of the time the deals are done in a couple

weeks to a month, but Carlos needs a little wiggle room. I think we'll see our money well before ninety days."

"Where do I sign?"

"Right across from where Carlos signed. You can see his signature was witnessed by his wife Marcella and by me. I'll also witness your signature and I'll get the receptionist Francene in here as a second witness. There are three copies: one for you, one for Carlos, and one for the Recorder's Office."

Antonio signed, followed by Manny and then Francene. "Don't go away," Manny said to the receptionist. "This last doc also has three copies. It's a deed of trust on the estate which guarantees the loan. If Carlos doesn't pay back the loan in accordance with its terms, this is the vehicle which allows you to take the estate in lieu of the payment."

Antonio perused the paper and noting that Carlos and his witnesses had already signed, put his signature on it. Manny and Francene followed.

"This pile is yours," Manny said, as he put a rubber band around the thick bunch of papers and handed them to Antonio.

"Thanks, that was very efficient. What do I do now?"

"We do business with a little insurance company in Lubbock, Texas. The money from all the investors goes there, and they send it on when we give them the go ahead. They don't ask questions and they're ecstatic to have their hands on eighty million dollars for a week or two."

Manny reached in his briefcase and pulled out a piece of yellow legal paper. Written on it was the name, Cattlemen's Life & Casualty Insurance Company, followed by a routing number and an account number. "Give your guy at Merrill Lynch a call and have him verify that these numbers belong to this company, then have him wire the ten and a half million."

Antonio used the phone on the conference table while Manny listened. "Done," Antonio said as he hung up.

"Perfect," Manny said. "As soon as I get a confirmation that the transfer was received, I'll give you a call and I'll record the documents."

Antonio got up and shook Manny's hand. "I'll wait for your call," he said as scooped up his pile of documents and headed for the door.

As soon as Antonio was out of sight, Manny took the other two sets of documents and ran them through the shredder along with all the other papers from his desk. He removed the few remaining personal items from his office and slid them into his briefcase and then he too headed for the door. "Thanks for your help, Francene," he said, as he walked out and retired from the loan brokerage business.

CHAPTER 50

O mar had already left for Miami where he would catch a commercial flight back to San Jose. Everyone else was on board the Citation. This time Manny took the seat behind the cockpit, Enrique and Marcella, and Annie and Carmen sunk into the soft middle seats, Brett occupied the right co-pilot seat, and of course Rob, the pilot in command, took his spot in the left seat. Brett turned to him, "You okay doing the check list by yourself? I have a couple calls to make."

"No problem. I'll start up the air conditioner but I'll wait till you're done before starting the engines."

Brett located the phone number for Connecticut Mutual Life in San Francisco and dialed it up. "Ralph

Phillips, please. This is Brett Raven, he's expecting my call."

"Brett, looks like you pulled it off," Ralph said, as soon as he picked up the phone.

"It arrived safe and sound?" Brett asked.

"Two hours ago. Ten and a half million. I can't wait to see the looks on those young lawyers' faces who tried to nix your deal."

"I'm not that interested in the glory. I'm more concerned that all the people who helped me get paid."

"Don't worry about that. I'll have the ten percent recovery fee released this afternoon. Should I send it through Vince Moreno?"

"That'll be fine. Give him a call; I won't be back in California until tonight."

"I'll do that and by the way, good job. I have no idea how you did it and I don't want to know. I do know, however, it just may get me a promotion."

"You deserve it, thanks for all your help. Send me your new business card when you get it," Brett added, and hung up.

Brett pulled a card out of his briefcase and dialed the number in California. A gruff voice answered, "Biff Erskine."

"Hey, Biff, guess who?"

"Raven, the fuck you want. Those goons of yours almost killed me."

"Yeah, but I ended up saving you, didn't I?"

"Well… thanks for that. Why're you calling me? I'm off the case"

"That's too bad because I've decided to give you

the information you wanted."

Biff was skeptical, "Why would you do that?"

"Because, actually I like you, and I want you to get that $100,000 bonus."

"So what's the deal? You give me his name and address and I just go and pick him up?"

"That depends on how fast you can get to Florida. I'm pretty sure he'll be on the run, so you'll actually have to earn that money."

"Something tells me you're screwing me over, but what the hell, give me the info."

"I'm not screwing you over, trust me. Do you have a pencil?" Brett asked.

"Yeah, go ahead."

"Antonio and Maria Russ, 27 Everglade Court, West Palm Beach Florida."

"That's it?" Biff asked.

"That's it, buddy. Good luck."

Brett glanced over at Rob who was waiting to get the jet engines started. He raised his right index finger. "One more call," he said.

He pushed a speed dial on his cell and the call was answered on the first ring. "Manny?" the voice asked eagerly.

"I'm afraid Manny won't be calling," Brett answered.

There was a pause on the other end while J.T. tried to figure out what was happening. Finally he said, "Who, who is this?"

"You might say it's an old friend back from the dead."

Again there was no response from the other end, just silence. Brett didn't say a word, waiting for J.T. to recover. Finally J.T. said, "Brett?"

"Are you surprised?"

"Well, yes, how is everything? How's Annie?"

"What if I told you she was dead? Would that surprise you?"

"I don't know what you mean?"

"Cut the crap, J.T., you know exactly what I mean. I can't believe we used to be friends. As far as I'm concerned you deserve to be thrown out with yesterday's garbage. It was my pleasure to bring you down."

"Bring me down?" he said, still not grasping the situation.

"I thought you might like to know that Cattlemen's Life & Casualty Insurance Company doesn't launder money for drug dealers. They're owned by a larger company, Connecticut Mutual Life. Does that name ring a bell?" No response, just more silence. Brett waited, allowing time for a tight knot to form in J.T.'s stomach. Finally Brett broke the silence. "That's one of the companies you defrauded. They were kind enough to allow Cattlemen's to receive a wire transfer from your Merrill Lynch account and that money is on its way back to them and the other two companies as we speak. I'm sure the fact that you personally authorized the transfer of the $10.5 million out of your own brokerage account will sit well with the judge."

"Judge, what judge?"

"The one you'll be standing before someday soon."

J.T.'s brain was finally processing the situation. "Why, why did you do this to me?"

"You really don't know, do you? Well, you're not going to have much time to figure it out. A four hundred pound private investigator named Biff Erskine is on his way from California to bring you back for the reward. You've got about a twelve hour head start. By the way, Annie and I hope you liked the photos we sent you. Sorry they weren't very pretty; we were having a bad hair day."

Brett flipped the cover shut on his cell phone and looked over at Rob who was waiting patiently. He gave him a thumbs up as he put on his headset and hit the intercom-on switch.

Rob started both engines and while waiting for them to spool up, turned toward Brett and keyed his mic. "Thanks for the great adventure, doc. How about giving ground control a call for a clearance and let's go home?"

My Thanks

_____

To *Candyce Griswold* and *Bev Paull* for their editing skills and hours of hard work.

To *Carla Resnick* for her creative design of the cover and contents.

To busy authors, *J.R. Hafer* and *Jamie Dodson*, for their time reading and praising the manuscript.

About The Author

Mike Paull is a retired dentist from the San Francisco Bay Area and is also a licensed commercial pilot with over thirty-five hundred flying hours.
He now resides in Chico, California.

Mike's first book, *Tales from the Sky Kitchen Café*, was published in 2011.

Flight of Betrayal, published in 2012, is the first of the Brett Raven mystery series.

Flight of Deception, published in 2013, is the second in the Brett Raven Trilogy

Follow the Brett Raven Mysteries

Facebook
Brett Raven Mysteries

Skyhawk Publishing
skyhawkpublishing.com

E-book format available
Amazon.com
Barnes and Noble.com
Apple Store.com

CPSIA information can be obtained at www.ICGtesting.com
Printed in the USA
LVOW12s0706030913

350646LV00001B/1/P